Sweden Calling

R. M. Mc[illegible]

Sweden Calling

L.M. McArthur

LMD Publishing

Published by LMD Publishing

Cover design by Usama Zaheen

Printed and bound in Great Britain by Clays Ltd.

ISBN: 978-1-0683866-0-2

I would like to thank everyone that has helped me with my book: from editing to typesetting, advice and words of wisdom. It's been much appreciated. Thank you.

Thanks, Iain, for always supporting me.

To Ryan and Abbie, I love you both very much. If I could give you one bit of advice it would be this. Never shrink yourself to fit in, with small minds and small places, keep growing it's a big world out there. You'll find your place and your people, I promise.

Lastly to the reader. Thank you for buying my book, I hope you like it and, if anything, I hope it makes you smile for a while.

Contents

Chapter One

May 1998

I pound the streets of Belfast, with the spring sun warming my back. Tomorrow, my Da will be coming to pick me and my friend Rochelle up, to take us back home to Cobh for the summer. I can't help but feel excited for what the months ahead will bring. It feels like a good time to be Irish, now that the Good Friday agreement was reached last month at Stormont. It's hard to believe that these streets of Belfast have seen more blood and violence than most cities – hopefully once and for all, everyone can live in peace. I look down once more at the cobbled streets below my feet and can't help imagining gruesome images. As quick as they come into my head, they leave again. I remind myself how lucky I was growing up in Southern Ireland and not Northern Ireland. Back when I was young it felt like two different worlds, the north and south. If the governments and paramilitary groups weren't working towards peace, my parents would never have let me come here to study.

I walk further along to the crossing that is just around the corner to my flat and I hear a wolf whistle just as I'm about to press the button for the traffic system. It stops me in my tracks before I can press the button. I look to the left and right of me, but there is no one there and I'm conscious I'm not going to be that girl that turns around to a whistle. It's probably workmen whistling to a woman behind me, I think.

"Oi Chelle!"

Oh, dear god that's my name, and I get a flashback to last weekend snogging some random guy in the pub. I choose to continue walking and pretend I never heard my name being called, now slightly quickening my pace.

"Chelle!" I feel a tug of my arm before I start to turn around and see Peter standing in front of me.

"Oh. Hey. How are you? Sorry I never heard you there," I say with a smile.

"I thought it was you," he says with a flash of a smile.

"How are you doing, Peter?" I ask.

"Am grand. Are you going out tonight? Everyone's going. It's the summer end of term leaving do," Peter says with a bit too much enthusiasm for my liking.

"Yeah if I'm feeling better. I was gonna go with Rochelle. What about you?" I ask quickly, trying to deflect and give limited information.

"Of course. Where you off to?" he asks, looking down at my bags of shopping.

"I'm just walking back to my flat." I point past Peter across the road, the house that stands out from all the rest with the purple door.

"Come on, I will walk you," he says while grabbing my shopping bags out of my hand, not giving me time to protest.

"Jesus! Who picked that colour for a front door?" Peter asks with a horrified expression on his face.

"I know, right? Me and Rochelle still say that every time we turn the key to our place. Who the feck chose that colour. We finally found out one night when we met the landlord, she's very eccentric, I think an old hippy. We were too scared to ask her, but I'm positive it was her," I laugh as I explain.

As I arrive at my door, Peter turns and hands me back my shopping bags. I thank him and tell him I might see him tonight. As I turn to close the door, I start to feel a bit bad as I've snogged Peter a few times when Rochelle and I have been out. I know he's keener on me than I am him. He is a nice guy though all the same. I just feel he tries a bit too hard at times. Plus, I'm having the best time of my life just now being young, wild, and free, the last thing I want is a boyfriend. For the last nine months since starting my first year at the Queen's University of Belfast, I don't have nagging parents telling me what time to get up or to tidy my room. I can lie all day in bed and be as happy as a "pig in shit" as the saying goes. My life is going well, and I don't need the hassle or complications of a man in my world right now. As my mother says, there's plenty of time for that carry on.

I close the door behind me and start kicking my shoes off. I can hear singing coming from upstairs – Rochelle must be home, I didn't think she was getting home till later. I shout up to her, trying to get my voice heard over the stereo blasting out the lyrics to Oasis' 'Maybe' and her singing over the top of it. I quickly climb the stairs and just then the volume of the stereo and Rochelle's singing hits me.

"Christ, Rochelle. Don't give up your day job. Jesus," I say with a sarcastic tone and half laugh.

Rochelle reaches over and turns the volume down. "You took your time, what's in the bags?"

"Oh, I got myself some makeup and a dress for tonight."

"Nice. Let's see the dress."

I take the dress out of the Miss Selfridge bag and hold it up to Rochelle. I then put it against me and twirl to the left and right. It's a baby doll style dress with chunky short sleeves just below my shoulders, the top part of the dress is cut almost square looking. The dress itself is black but when you lift the layer of mesh up its bright blue underneath and catches the light when you move for the blue to shine through.

"That's nice, Chelle. I like it – how much did that cost you?" Rochelle asks.

"Twenty-three ninety-nine. I thought it was a bargain. Think I'm going to wear it tonight. What about you?" I ask.

"I've white trousers, I'm going to wear it with a little red top," Rochelle says.

"Sounds nice. Guess what? You'll never guess who I met when I was walking back: Peter! He asked if I was going tonight. I said I wasn't feeling great, but I might go," I say pulling a face.

"Jeez. He's keen," Rochelle laughs.

I make sure Rochelle has started her packing for My Da coming tomorrow to collect us. He needs to make the round trip from Cobh to Belfast and back and the last thing he will want to do is wait for us all day. Everything is mostly packed for tomorrow. My room looks very sparse. I have to strip my bed tomorrow and my makeup that is on my dresser, apart from that all my cases and bags are all over in the far corner beside the window ready to go. I lay my new dress on the bed and rummage through my case to find a pair of heels that will go with it. After I find a pair I like, I plug in my straighteners so that by the time I've had my shower they will be hot enough to do something with my thick, light brown hair. I decided not to wash my hair, as I just washed it this morning and can't be bothered doing it all over again. After being in the shower for what feels like an eternity, I open the door, and the steam comes out before I do.

"Jesus Chelle. I thought you were dead in there. I hope you've left me some hot water," Rochelle says with a laugh watching the steam descend from the bathroom.

"I have, don't worry."

Once we are both ready, Rochelle says she is going to go and get some drinks and snacks from the corner shop and use the payphone.

"I better call my folks. They will be putting out a search party, I haven't called home in a few days," Rochelle says walking out the door.

While Rochelle is away, I tidy around the flat, so that there is less to do in the morning. Out of the two of us, I'm less messy. I go and have a sneak peak in Rochelle' room to ensure she has started packing, as I'm not wanting my Da to give me grief when he's got to wait ages. To my surprise she is all packed. *She must be missing home as much as I am*, I think to myself.

A short while later I hear the door closing from downstairs.

"What's wrong, Rochelle?" I can tell from the look on my friend's face that something is wrong.

Rochelle just bursts into tears and it's hard to make out what she is trying to tell me.

"It's my Gran... she's passed. She passed yesterday. They were going to wait and tell me sure, when I got home tomorrow, but my sister told me on the phone," Rochelle says through tears.

I give her a hug; she cuddles me back and puts her head on my shoulder.

"Come get a seat, Rochelle," I say while guiding her to the big sofa in the living room.

I sit with Rochelle some more in silence. After a while, she composes herself.

"Chelle, I'm not going to go out tonight. The last thing I want to do is go out and have fun and talk to people. I'm just going to sit here if that's okay. You go out though and enjoy yourself. I would just be awful company," she says quietly.

"Absolutely not. I'm going to stay here with you. I'm not letting you sit here by yourself," I say in a forceful tone.

"Honestly Chelle, I don't mind. It's the end of year party, you should go, I will be fine," she says eagerly.

"No and that's the end of it. There will always be next year, plus you and I could do with a night in with all the drink we have consumed these last few months," I say trying to be funny and make Rochelle smile.

I put on the TV and get us a duvet, juice and crisps just to slouch on the couch. Just so my friend knows I'm right here for her if she needs anything. I pour us a glass of Fanta each.

"Thanks Chelle. You're a good friend," Rochelle says with a smile.

Chapter Two

"Hurry up Chelle! I've been shouting you for the last twenty minutes."

I give a yawn and a stretch and think to myself, *I suppose I'd better get up*. It feels like a thought to move from this warm bed. I'm nice and cozy and as soon as I pull these covers off me the cold is going to hit me. Now, all I can hear is my Ma blasting the hoover downstairs; there's always someone about to disturb my peace and quiet. You don't get any peace in this house.

After I've made my bed, I lay out my work clothes and head on in for a shower, even though I still have a raging hangover from the night before. I feel like I am still at Uni, with nights out on the tiles, but I'm not. I've been back at home living for the last two weeks, to get much needed money together for my second year. Although, the way I'm going with my nights out, I won't have anything saved by the time Uni starts again in September. McLafferty's takes on students from all over Europe for a working holiday to work in their restaurants. At night, the upstairs restaurant comes alive and lots of tourists pay a fee to watch and listen to Irish folk music and dancing, while also enjoying their meal.

Oh sugar, the time. I quickly fix my hair.

"Chelle, here's some brekkie for ya," Ma shouts just as I'm about to head out the door.

"Nah Ma, it's fine, I've not got time, will see you later. Thanks though."

I run down the road, constantly checking my watch. I am almost sprinting around by the harbour and, before I know it, I'm running through the main restaurant doors of my work.

"Sorry," I shout to my supervisor Cath on my way to the back stairs.

I can hear a lot of laughter coming from the staff room. I hate going into the staff room when there's lots of people, especially when it's all summer staff talking in different languages, it makes me feel self-conscious. I often wonder if they're talking about me. Especially if I'm on a break and there is just myself and two others from say France and they are talking back and forth. I know I shouldn't think of myself as being *soo* important – they are probably talking about the weather or something – it just makes me feel awkward. I walk into the staff cloakroom first, to hang up my jacket and plan on popping my head into the staff room to see who's about. As I'm turning to leave to go into the next room, I hear a stranger say hello.

I turn to face the voice. Oh, dear god, I think I've died and gone to heaven.

"Erm... hello," I say, stumbling over my words.

"I'm Mattias, nice to meet you."

"Hi! I'm Michelle, nice to meet you, too."

I can feel my face getting redder and redder.

"This is my first day, I'm the new waiter – I'm here for the season," he says with a very warm, welcoming smile in excellent English.

"Really nice to meet you. I better go, I'm running late. Bye."

I dart out of the door, nearly taking the door off its hinges and run back downstairs, forgetting to even go and have a nosey in the staff room.

Downstairs, I get instructions from Cath to start stacking the dishes in the dishwasher. While I'm stacking the plates, I can't help but think about what just happened up the stairs. I never get embarrassed. I'm usually quite outgoing, not ballsy or that, but confident enough. I replay his image over and over in my mind while working. He was tall, about 6 feet, with lovely sallow, sunkissed skin. His light brown hair flopped down over his eyes slightly. He had the bluest of eyes and a sharp, chiseled jawline, looking as though he had walked straight out of a catwalk. *I wonder where he's from*. I consider the thought over in my head and find myself guessing. My money is a Scandinavian country. I catch myself having a full-blown conversation with myself in my head about where this sexy stranger is from.

After I stack the dishes, I go through and ask Cath what else needs to be done before the lunch time rush.

"Can you go up to the upstairs kitchen and ask them if they have the Irish stew and beef stroganoff ready?" she asks.

"Sure, Cath, no probs," I reply.

I hurry up the stairs and try my hardest to stop myself from laughing. Yes, I've got an excuse to see the handsome stranger again.

My friend Rochelle works here too, but she's not on 'till three today – I can't wait to fill her in.

"Hi erm... Hi Mattias," I say shyly.

It's only him in the kitchen. I'm not sure where the rest of them are but I'm more than happy with it only being him and me in this kitchen. He can't hear me because he has Ireland's own Boyzone playing, All I need. I march on up to him.

"Hello Mattias."

"Hello again, Michelle, what can I do for you?"

"Oh, I can think of a few things you could do for me," I think to myself.

"Cath has sent me up because she's wondering if the Irish stew and beef stroganoff are ready?"

"Yes, Jacob has prepared them both and has left them over there for someone to take downstairs. But now that you're here I shall give you some help to take them back downstairs," he says sincerely.

"Thanks," I say with a flash of a smile.

We start loading the food onto the trolley. He wheels everything round to the small lift and puts it in for me.

"Will you be okay with it when it's downstairs?"

"Aye, I will be fine, it's just a case of wheeling it through."

Before I know it, I come straight out with it.

"Sure, look at you, the proper gent. You wanna come out for a drink tonight with me and ma friends?"

"Sorry – slow down, you talk too fast," he says laughing with a puzzled expression on his face.

"Do you want to come out tonight with me and my friends for a drink?" I repeat.

"Yes, what time shall I meet you and where?"

I look up and now see his piercing blue eyes staring at me. I hold his gaze for a second, before breaking eye contact.

"Shall we say eight o'clock at Connelly's pub?"

"Will I find it okay?"

Just at that moment, Jacob walks in.

"Will you find what okay, Mattias?" Jacob asks, raising his brows.

I interject. "Connelly's pub."

"Christ. You can't get lost in this town, Mattias, it's tiny," Jacob shouts.

The suspense is killing me, so I have to ask him.

"By the way, where are you from, Mattias?"

He gives me a curious smile before answering, "Why?"

"I'm just being nosey and curious, that's all," I say softly.

"Sweden – Stockholm to be exact."

I smile and raise my eyebrows.

"Any more questions for me, Miss Michelle?"

Before I can think or answer, Jacob butts in. "Right you two, come on get moving, we've got work to do," he tells us sternly.

Mattias' face changes from smiling to serious. I suppose his boss has spoken and I better not get him into trouble, it is his first day after all. Jacob is the supervisor of the upstairs restaurant.

The afternoon quickly flies in and before I know it, Rochelle has started her shift. The self-service has been very busy. Cath has had me out clearing the tables as the dishes that have been piling up. Rochelle is on the hot counter serving. I need to get a hold of her. I take a trolley load of dishes into old Mary (who should have retired years ago but continues to work and sings while she does the dishes).

"Mary Doll, there's another load for ya," I say.

"Oh aye, why are you so happy Michelle?"

"Have you not seen the hunky Swedish man up the stairs Mary? He's eye candy for ya" I exclaim and hear my voice getting higher pitched with excitement.

"Oh, the bloody foreigner! You be careful, he'll get the knickers off you then run away," warns old Mary.

With a stern tone, she then proceeds to tell me how she's worked there for thirty years and has seen loads of "that carry on over the years."

"Those foreigners, they come over here for the season and

they have their wicked way, then feck off back home. Sure now, be careful," she tells me.

"Calm down, Mary!"

Mary is your typical old lady of a certain age, who has never left Ireland but has an opinion on everything and everyone. She means well and does have a good heart but typically the way she says things comes out highly offensive, but does she care? No, not one bit. If she's got something to say it's going to come out. No matter who she offends.

I walk off while Mary is still talking, I'm not sure if she's talking to me or to herself and decide now is the time to sneak back out to the self-service and try and catch Rochelle' attention.

"Rochelle, have you been up the stairs to the kitchen and seen the new waiter?"

"No. I've not had a chance to move from here since I came in," complains Rochelle. "Why, am I missing something?" she asks, raising her eyebrows up and down, with a giggle.

"Yeah, he's fit as hell. I've asked him to come for a drink with us tonight," I smile.

The day passes quickly and before I know it, it's come to the end of my shift. I don't hang about. I run to get my jacket to go straight home and get ready for my date with Mr. Scandinavian tonight.

I don't even notice the walk back around the harbour and up the brae, by the time I come to my senses I'm back at home deciding what to wear in front of the mirror. *Hmm that's a maybe*, I think to myself and then toss it on top of the rest of the clothes I've flung on my bed and on the floor.

"Chelle. Your tea's getting cold down here, will you hurry up? We're all starving!" me Da shouts.

"Sorry Da, just coming, give me five minutes," I shout back.

I've got Ghetto Superstar blasting on my CD player. My family is quite chilled tonight considering, normally they're balling at me to turn the music down. Eventually I make my way down the stairs and into the dining room for tea, all my family just sitting there in silence, waiting for me as usual. Except my mum, she's busy talking to herself as she takes the food through from the kitchen.

"Jesus, Mary and Joseph, did you not eat at work today?" Ma says, gob smacked as I'm horsing down my spaghetti.

"Yea Ma, I did. I'm in a hurry to get out tonight with the girls," I say quickly, not lifting my eyes up off the plate.

My older sister Shannon pipes up. "She never eats her food as quick as this Ma, she's rushing cos she must have a man on the go."

"Shut it, Shannon, I do not."

Me Ma and Da then give each other a funny look. I get up to take my plate away as I can't sit all night gabbing back and forth, I've got other things on my mind... A date with a handsome stranger.

I've finally decided what I am wearing, having done one more twirl in the mirror before I head out. Bit bold all the same, for my small town in southern Ireland, but hell if Ginger Spice can get away with it so can Michelle Doyle from Cobh. I'm wearing a blue army style dress with slits up the side that just comes to my knee. The dress is full length and to top it off, platform trainers. I take out my straighteners, every girl's best friend. Especially if they have wiry, curly hair. I straighten my hair as best as I can. I was almost tempted to straighten my hair again with an iron but after the last time, I don't think I will be doing that again in a hurry. A few of the girls and me at uni did it one night after one too many drinks and I burnt my head, thankfully my hair wasn't singed.

I rush out the door shouting on my way, "See you later, don't stay up. Bye, love you." I make sure I leave quickly so as not to get the Spanish inquisition from my parents.

Chapter Three

I get to Connelly's pub just about quarter to eight when I see the girls waiting for me – Roisin, and Cara.

"Is Rochelle not with you?" asks Roisin.

"No, she's getting here later, after work." I look past them to the pub door.

"Do you know if he's here yet?"

"We don't know what he looks like, Chelle," Cara states matter of fact.

"Believe me, girls, you will know him the moment you see him," I assure them.

I open the big wooden doors at Connelly's and hold it for the other two girls to go in first. Once inside, I glance around the bar but he's not in yet. I feel a bit disappointed inside, thinking that he's not going to come. Cara orders the three of us a drink: vodka and Coke all round. We go and find a booth near the door so we can see who's coming in and out.

Connelly's is not too big a pub, the bar is in a circle, and you can walk all the way around it, there's the beer garden section outside and private little booths all dotted about inside.

Like all pubs it has that stale cigarette and beer smell to it. I bob my head to Janet Jackson's song 'Together Again' playing on the shiny jukebox nearby and glance at the tv screens above the bar, all tuned to MTV but with the sound down.

It's almost twenty past eight and I've now started my second vodka. The girls are chatting between themselves, but I can't seem to hear what they are saying as my mind is too preoccupied. I feel flat inside, but my stomach is turning also. I've not completely let go to the glimmer of hope that he will still walk through the door. On one hand I can't stop thinking he's not going to show and on the other, there's still time. I turn to say something to Cara and Roisin but just at that moment he walks in, with another of the workers from McLafferty's.

"Hi, over here, Mattias!" I shout over the music blasting in the background and frantically wave my hands.

I catch his eye and he eventually sees me waving, then gives me a wave back. He proceeds to start walking over with the other guy following his lead. They both come straight over and sit down beside us.

"Sorry, I didn't get away from the tables on time," Mattias explains.

"Oh, that's okay, you're here now. These are my friends, Cara and Roisin," I say with a smile.

They both lean over the table to shake his hand, and I can tell by the smile on Roisin's face that she likes what she sees.

Roisin is a beauty. She is tall and pale but with interesting features and sleek ginger hair that she dyes a vibrant red. Some would say all the features of your typical Irish woman.

"Hi girls, nice to meet you. This is my friend Martin, he's German and is over here for the summer also," says Mattias.

The three of us say hello to Martin. Mattias asks us all if we want a drink.

Before I can respond, Cara says, "Nah, you're fine Mattias, we've got some thanks."

The girls sit chatting to Martin. I'm getting the vibe that Roisin likes Martin also; she's appearing to be staring at him intently, taking in his every word. Cara has an on-off boyfriend called Daniel. Just now they seem to be on again. Cara's hair catches the light in the pub with all her blonde highlights reflecting in the light. She's naturally dark brown but gets blonde highlights in her hair to lighten it. She is about my height, five foot six and half an inch. The half an inch is very important.

"Cara, the light is reflecting off your highlights," I say then everyone has a look and feels Cara's hair which has a wave in it.

After we've all had a feel of Cara's hair, I turn to Mattias and start chatting to him. I keep all my focus on Mattias, as he does me. Anybody could be trying to talk to us right now and we wouldn't have a clue.

"So, have you lived in Stockholm all your life?"

"Yes, I've lived there all my life. I live in the suburbs of Stockholm."

We chat for what seems to be ages about Sweden, Ireland, family and music and the more he talks the more I loosen up and become more at ease in his company. Sometime later Rochelle arrives.

"Hey," Rochelle says to everyone.

"Hi, we met earlier at work," Mattias says.

Rochelle squeezes into the booth and starts chatting to everyone. I look over and notice Roisin and Martin are getting very touchy feely with one another.

The vodka and tequila shots are in full flow, and this seems evenly so, as everyone is shouting over one another. Madonna's 'Ray of Light' comes on and I really want to dance to it, especially now the vodka is kicking in. I start pulling and hauling

Mattias up onto the dance floor. Once we get on the dance floor, I'm really going for it with my arms and legs going in every direction. After a few shots, who doesn't think they're the best dancer to hit the dance floor? I look over at Mattias and he's busting a few moves too. He's a good dancer, I'm impressed! And you know what they say about men who can dance.

Roisin and Martin are snogging the face off one another on the dance floor. Cara is over at the bar now getting cozy with her on off boyfriend Daniel and poor Rochelle is sitting by herself.

"Hey, let's go back over and sit with Rochelle," I say.

"You're a good dancer," Mattias says with a smile.

"You're not too bad yourself," I reply.

As we get over to the booth, I see Rochelle looking fed up.

"I feel bad that you're sitting over here by yourself, so we came back over," I say.

"Oh, don't feel bad, I'm just eyeing up the talent," Rochelle laughs.

As quickly as she said it, Rochelle is up over at the bar talking to a guy.

Mattias offers to walk me home and gives me his jacket as he can see that my teeth are chittering.

"Your town is lovely, Michelle, you must be fit with all the hills you have to walk up every day," Mattias says.

"Oh, you get used to the hills. Better craic going down them than climbing up them," I giggle.

Just at that Mattias starts laughing.

"What's so funny?" I ask.

"You have funny words here, but I love your accent. What does craic mean?" He tilts his head quizzically.

"It means, fun, excitement or getting the latest gossip with your friends," I explain.

We stop at the top of the hill to catch our breath. Mattias can see down to the harbour. It's lovely at nighttime with all the lights reflecting off the bay. In the distance you can see the grand St Colman's Cathedral towering over the harbour. I turn around to say something and our eyes meet, the next thing I know, we are kissing. He puts his arm around me and pulls me in tighter. He starts stroking my hair. For a split second, I lose all inhibitions but quickly pull myself back to reality and remember that I would be the talk of the town for weeks if I don't get a check on myself. His kissing is skilled and confident, he starts kissing the side of my neck. It sends my body into a frenzy. Just at that moment, a taxi passes, bringing me once more back to my senses.

"I better go in now," I say flushed.

"Can I see you again, Michelle?" Mattias asks politely.

"Yes, I would like that," I smile.

"What time do you want to meet tomorrow? I'm on 'til finish."

"So am I. Well, until the tables leave."

McLafferty's doesn't close until ten and then there's the cleaning up so when you're on until you finish you don't usually get away till eleven pm.

"I will go and grab a shower and then come and get you at the staff accommodation if you want?" I ask.

"Yes, okay, I look forward to tomorrow," he responds. He leans down and kisses me on the lips once more.

I start walking away and after taking a few steps, I turn back to get one more glance at him. He looks back also and smiles at me.

"Mattias, call me Chelle or Shelly, all my friends and family call me that, Michelle' my Sunday name," I say with a laugh.

"Okay Chelle," he shouts and laughs back at me.

Chapter Four

I open the front door quietly to my house, but everyone is in bed. Sometimes, my sister Shannon is up, and we will sit and have a natter but I'm feeling a bit tipsy and a bit euphoric about tonight's events. While I brush my teeth, I smile looking at myself in the mirror replaying tonight's events over and over in my head.

The next morning, I check my alarm and can't believe I've slept until eleven am. I'm having a stretch in my bed to wake myself up, when I hear my mother shout, "Shelly, that's Roisin on the phone for you."

Oh, Christ. You never get five minutes peace. Someone's always shouting at you or wanting your attention in this house. I thump my feet onto the floor.

"Coming, Ma."

"Hey guess what? That Martin is a feckin ride and a half," squeals Roisin.

I can't stop laughing. Roisin says what she thinks and has no filter, the best nights out are always with Roisin.

"So, tell me more, I want to know all the juicy gossip," I exclaim in excitement!

There is always someone hanging about listening in my house. You can't get any privacy when you're on the phone because it's out in the hall and everyone can hear your conversation. I whisper quietly at times when me Ma or one of them walks past or I just stop abruptly until there's no nosey ears listening.

"Aye, well, I went back to the staff accommodation, and we were almost getting a bit frisky but then your man Mattias knocked on his door looking for him, so we stopped. I tell ya, I was pissed off. Mattias saw that I was there so he said he would come back later but the moment was gone Chelle, so I said it's okay, I'm just leaving. We've organised to see each other again tonight for round two," she says with the dirtiest of laughs.

Just at that moment there's laughter on the line.

"Is that you Kian? Get off the feckin phone. You're a nosey little shit," I shout to my younger brother who is fourteen and so annoying.

"Ma, tell Kian to get out of you and Da's room and stop listening to me and Roisin's phone call," I shout, feeling my anger rising.

My mother starts yelling at my brother.

"Listen I'm going to head and will see you tonight at Connelly's," I say flatly.

"Okay, cool. See you later Chelle."

The day passes quickly and before I know it, I'm starting my shift at McLafferty's. I walk into the staff room hoping to get a glimpse of Mr. Scandinavia, but no one is there. As if like Groundhog Day I once more hang up my jacket and head down to start my shift. Just as I'm heading down the stairs, who is coming up the stairs but sexy Scandinavian.

"Hey Mattias."

"Hello Chelle, how are you?"

"I'm good thanks. You?"

"All the better for seeing you."

I feel shy and try to think of something to say.

I blurt out, "So did you have a good night last night?"

"Yes, I did," he replies with a warm smile stretching over his face.

Having gone all tongue-tied and giddy, I only manage to muster, "Good."

He laughs. I think he knows I've gone shy.

"Well, I better get going, will see you tonight at Connelly's."

He smiles at me once more and I'm guessing trying to be funny he says, "Not if I see you later in here."

We've been mobbed all shift. I sometimes wonder where all the tourists come, from especially thirty minutes before closing, which can be a pain in the ass. All the bus parties we had in today were American and Japanese tourists. We were so busy, I didn't get up the stairs again to see Mattias. While mopping the floor, all I can think about is what am I going to wear tonight; will I wear my black trousers with my nice halter neck red top, heels, and my black denim jacket? Or one of my many dresses? *Decisions, decisions,* I think to myself. I don't want to go too dressy because Cobh isn't a city and I don't want Mattias to think I am trying too hard, even though I am.

I get to Connelly's and Roisin, Martin and Mattias are already sitting in the same booth that we all sat in last night, waiting for me.

"Alright, how's everyone tonight?" I ask.

Mattias gets up and gives me a kiss on both checks and whispers, "You look nice."

I can feel my stomach jumping already.

"Thanks."

I turn to sit down, and Roisin gives me a cheeky smile.

"What would you like to drink, Chelle?" Mattias asks.

"Can I just get a vodka and coke please?"

Mattias comes back later with a drink for everyone. Roisin is talking away to Martin, and I sit speaking to Mattias. He tells me that his parents have split up and that he has two brothers and a sister. His sister is the eldest, then Mattias and his two younger brothers. I ask him lots of questions about Sweden and of course, Abba! I love Abba! At uni we would organise nights to go around the bars in Belfast and at the end of the night when everyone was bleary eyed and the worse for wear, the last bar of the night would always be a karaoke bar and blast out good old Abba tunes. Who the hell doesn't like Abba?

"So, what do you do at uni, Chelle?" Mattias asks intrigued.

"I'm studying sales and marketing at uni. I'm just going into my second year, then after that I will have another two years left of study."

"Will you stay in Belfast after you qualify?"

"I'm not sure, I may go travelling. I haven't thought that far ahead. What about you, what brought you to Ireland?"

"I wanted to see a bit of the world as I'm young, I'm only twenty-one and love being a waiter. It's great that you can go anywhere in the world."

As Mattias is talking to me I'm looking attentively at him. The light in the bar is very bright and shows up on his face. He has the most beautiful skin with not one blemish or spot and the most amazing white teeth. All Europeans seem to have lovely teeth. It's the Irish and the British that don't have great teeth.

"What, what is it, Chelle?" Mattias catches me admiring him a bit too much. I'm oblivious as I'm away in a world of my own, until his voice brings me back to my senses.

"Nothing." *I'm just admiring you*, I think to myself.

I'm suddenly aware that I've been staring at him a little too much and that he noticed. I make a mental note in my mind; I need to be less obvious next time.

Mattias' last comment resonates with me. "I've never thought of it that way before but you're right. Doesn't matter where in the world you are, everyone will visit a restaurant. You picked a good job then, to see the world," I say sincerely.

I feel like I've not spoken to Roisin all night. Her and Martin appear only to have eyes for each other, most of the night they've had their tongues down each other's throat.

She appears to come up for air. "Chelle have you said to Mattias about next Saturday?"

Before I can say anything Mattias jumps in with, "What's happening next Saturday?" and then turns swiftly round to me.

"It's Chelle's twenty first birthday and her Ma and Da are having a party for her," Roisin jumps in before I can answer. "You and Martin should come along."

"Yes, of course, I would love to," Mattias says.

"Well, it's only a few of my family and friends, it's at my house and you're more than welcome to come along. Me Ma will probably bore you with all the questions she will have for you all."

"I will try and see if I can finish early that day in the restaurant," Mattias says.

"Great. Just tell Jacob I've invited you to my party."

The drinks are going down well, I look at the table and see all our empty glasses. The music comes on and the four of us are up on the dance floor dancing to all the cheesy classics. YMCA and I Will Survive. Brandy's new song comes on – 'Almost Doesn't Count.' I start dancing close to Mattias and the closer I dance next to him, the more I can feel my body tingle.

The barman shouts last orders, before anyone decides to get

another drink. I turn to Mattias. I'm tired and want to head off home. Mattias agrees with me. We say our goodbyes to the others and Mattias starts to walk me home.

Once we get to my gate I thank him for a nice night. The wind is blowing on my face and my hair is going everywhere. He smiles and strokes my hair away from my face and tells me he had a nice night too. He leans down and kisses me and, jeezo, my stomach is doing butterflies and I have that nice warm feeling inside.

"Goodnight Mattias."

Our hands linger, pulling away from each other. We both walk slightly backwards, not wanting the night to end.

"Goodnight, Chelle, see you tomorrow."

"I'm off tomorrow, so I won't see you at work."

"I finish at five o'clock tomorrow. Do you want to meet me about six o'clock?" he says.

"Yes, I will meet you then."

Just as I've answered him, he pulls me back to him and then leans in and kisses me once more, putting his hands through my hair and sending my body wild with desire.

Chapter Five

As soon as my alarm goes off, I'm up and about and make my way into town for a walk. I've got a bit of time to kill 'till I meet Rochelle for lunch. I have a wander around some of the shops (not that there's many in my wee town) there is a lady's clothing shop and a few other shops for tourists. You know the ones I mean, that you get in all holiday towns and then the hundreds of charity shops, I think it's the same everywhere, and it's especially so in Cobh.

While I'm having a look round the clothing shop, Madonna's 'Ray of Light' comes on playing over the radio. I suddenly have a flashback to dancing around like a looney the other night and let out a laugh to myself. The woman in the shop looks up and gives me a funny look. I try on a few bits and pieces. The dress I'm trying on is nice, it's like a tie dye light green and yellow and it goes just above my knee. It's a size ten, I've lost a bit of weight since I've been at Uni; not getting my ma's good old home cooking, I think that's what's done it. My figure looks good in this even if I do say so myself. Sold.

I check my watch – it's ten to one and I think I better get a move on or I will be late meeting Rochelle. She's always punctual – if you say one o'clock it's guaranteed she will always be there ten to fifteen minutes early, whatever time you arrange to meet. I am usually the opposite and chasing my tail wherever I go.

Sure enough, there's Rochelle sitting waiting for me at the window. We wave to each other.

"Hey, how are you?" I reach in and give her a hug.

"Yea good thanks, Chelle, how's you?"

"I'm good, I've got loads to tell you about the hunky Scandinavian."

"Oh, I can't wait to hear all."

We both order some cheese and ham toasties and carry on nattering.

"So enough about me, tell me about you. Have you got anyone on the go?" I ask.

"Nah, I can't be arsed with men just now. I really like Anthony from Uni. Will see how that goes when we go back in September, as he's away back home to Dublin for the break."

Rochelle is doing the same course as me, and we have been lifelong friends since we first started school at five years old. Rochelle took a shine to Anthony last year. He goes to the same university as us, but he stays in the halls of residence.

Just then our toasties arrive and with the smell of them I start to feel quite hungry. Rochelle pipes up, "The salad and garnish at the side looks too good to eat."

"Aye it does but I'm starving, I'm going to devour the lot."

After lunch we say our goodbyes and agree to meet up with the other girls on Saturday night.

"Okay, will see you tomorrow in work, Chelle."

"No, you won't. I'm off tomorrow as well, not back 'till Saturday late shift."

"Okay, see you Saturday."

I start making the long walk around the bay then up the big hill, back to my house. Once home I plonk myself down on the chair and recline it as far as it will go. I get myself all comfy and start watching tv with me Da. Just as I'm starting to relax my younger brother comes bounding in full of energy.

"Da the boxing is on tomorrow night, gonna get it out?" Kian says at the top of his lungs.

"Who's fighting?" my Da asks as he picks his head up from the paper he's reading.

"Prince Nazeem."

"Ay will get it on Sky, I like him."

"Thanks, Da, is it okay if two of my pals come over and watch it?"

"Aye, sure no bother son."

"Cheers Da."

Just as quickly as he came through the doors, Kian was gone again.

"Right Da, I'm away to get ready. I've been sitting here too long," I say, struggling to get off the recliner.

"How, where you off to?"

"I'm meeting my friend at six, Da," I say impatiently.

"You're no having tea? Your Ma will be annoyed," my Da, says surprised.

"I will definitely join you all tomorrow," I nod.

"Okay darlin," me Da says, giving me a smile then burying his head back down to the paper. The crossword seems to hold all his attention.

When I get up to my room, I put my music on full pelt – Mariah Carey's 'Honey' song. I put it on repeat as I love that song. I tend to do that with songs when they first come out in the charts, I constantly play them and then I end up sickening myself of them. I think my parents are getting deaf as they haven't shouted up once to turn it down. It's usually my little brother that does the moaning now.

"Turn that crap off," is what usually comes out of his mouth.

If my father catches him swearing and blinding then all hell breaks loose, he starts cursing, to which my mother will pipe in.

"Well Patrick, how do you expect him to learn when he's hearing you swearing," is usually my mother's answer.

Finally, I'm ready: just applying my lipstick and that's me and its only quarter to six, which is good by my standards. I check myself one more time in the mirror before I head out, my hair's gone wavy tonight and so typical. I hate my hair when it does that. Straighteners just don't straighten my hair properly.

"Bye," I shout while closing the door behind me as I go.

I head on down to the staff accommodation where I've to meet Mattias. Just as I'm walking around I look up at the staff accommodation and on the first floor I can see Mattias sitting by the window. He must be waiting for me – *Oh that's sweet*, I think to myself. Inside the building there are about twenty plus en-suite bedrooms. The owners of McLafferty's (a husband and wife) own the staff building as well as the restaurant. They run a youth hostel, and the rest of the rooms are used for the summer staff to stay in. They also get their meals free at the restaurant. I think they do live-in staff some sort of deal for staying rent and meal free.

I'm right outside the building and just about to buzz in, Mattias shouts out.

"Hello Chelle, I'm coming down just now,"

Before I can respond, he's gone from the window.

"How are you?" He leans in to give me a kiss.

"I'm good. Would you like to see a bit of Cobh?" I ask with flushed cheeks.

I can't take my eyes off his lips; they are so voluptuous and peachy. *How can one man be so good looking?* I think to myself.

"Yes, why not," he says in a warm tone and gives me a smile.

Mattias then proceeds to take me by the hand. I show him the local heritage centre, where we have a look around and I tell him about the local history: how Cobh is famous for being the last port the Titanic stopped at. The statue of Annie Moore and the story behind her. After looking around the heritage centre we walk to the local harbour and stop at the houses, which are all painted a different colour. Mattias takes out his disposable camera and takes plenty of photos along the way. He shouts to a passerby and asks them if they can take a photo of us; we stand at the railing with the sea at the back of us and he pulls me close, we both smile for the camera.

"Cheese."

Mattias laughs, "Why do you say cheese when you are getting your picture taken?"

"Sure, everyone says cheese," I reply.

Mattias laughs and I don't think he quite understands what I mean.

We walk back to the painted houses and there is a small park just across the road. We sit on the grass and talk some more.

"Have you stayed here all your life?" Mattias asks.

"Aye, I've stayed here all my days."

"It's very beautiful here and the people here have been so friendly."

"Aye! It's a nice wee town. Everybody knows everyone or you're related to half the town, but it's a good place to grow up."

"When I first told my mother that I was going to Ireland to work, she was quite worried just because of the troubles," he says with a serious face.

"Southern Ireland is fine; you get no bother here."

Mattias starts playing with my hair and I lean in to kiss him. His lips are soft and gentle. He has one hand around my back and his other hand balancing on the ground. After a while we stop kissing for some air and he pulls me to look at him.

"You are very beautiful, Chelle. I don't know what you are doing to me but I think you are driving me a little crazy," he says with a laugh.

I'm speechless, all I can do is give a coy smile.

"Do you want to come back to my accommodation?" he asks without a hint of shyness.

Inside I laugh to myself and before I can compose myself it's just straight out my mouth. "Yeah, okay."

We start walking to the accommodation back around the bay. I've never been in the staff flats before. His place is nice, not too small: he has a nice double bed and the big window makes the room look airy. There's a wardrobe, a chest of drawers and a chair by the window. He has two photos on his bedside cabinet, one photo is of him and his siblings and what looks like his mother, the other photo is him and an older man who looks the double of Mattias but only older. I presume it's his father.

Just as I'm sitting the photos back down, Mattias explains: "That's my mother, her name is Ingrid and that is my sister Annika and the two younger boys, they are my brothers Anders and Erik. The other photo is me and my father, his name is Filip."

"You have a good-looking family."

Mattias laughs.

"If you don't mind me asking Mattias, why did your mother and father split up?"

"He was cheating on my mother with another woman and my mother found out."

Mattias puts his head down and I feel a bit sorry for him;

you can clearly see it still hurts him. I shouldn't have asked him that question I think, and I start to feel a bit awkward.

"I'm sorry," is all I can manage to say.

"Don't be. It happened many years ago now when my youngest brother Erik was two. My mother hated him for a long time, but they get on fine now and she forgave him eventually. She moved on with her life a long time ago and has a good life now."

"That's good."

"He has always been a very good father to all of us. He was just a shitty husband to my mother."

He changes the subject and takes out a bottle of red wine.

"Would you like a drink?"

"Yes, go on then."

I walk over to the big chest of drawers and on top of them Mattias has a small CD player and loads of CDs. I start looking at his collection, he has everything there from Oasis to Robert Miles to Abba.

"Pick whatever you want, I love Britpop," he says leaning his head onto my shoulder.

Not wanting to look too cheesy, I pick 'You Get What You Give' by New Radicals.

"Oh, I like them," Mattias gives me a nod of approval.

As I sit at the window Mattias walks over to me and hands me my glass of wine. We sit there talking for ages about all sorts of things, the conversation is never forced and comes naturally, we both seem very interested in what the other has to say. I find myself at ease talking to him.

After a couple of refills, I find myself to be a little bit tipsy and have the hiccups. Mattias goes back up to the CD player and changes the music, this time he puts on The Verve – 'The Drugs Don't Work'. We start kissing, one thing leads to another, and I decide to stay a while longer.

Chapter Six

The next morning, I wake up later than I wanted to. *Oh shit!* I think to myself. My parents are going to be so pissed I didn't come home last night. I've never done that before. Mattias is still sleeping, he looks so peaceful. We are lying semi-clothed in bed together; he has his arm around me. As I look at the clock on the wall, he starts to stir from his sleep. It's seven am. I totally just lost track of time and must have fallen asleep.

Mattias wakes, I give him a kiss and get dressed. I tell him I better go home as I never told my parents I was staying out last night. Before I leave Mattias' room I go into his bathroom and splash my face with some water. He throws some clothes on and walks me to the outside door. We give each other a cuddle and say our goodbyes for now and organise to meet later.

As I leave the accommodation, the place is still like a ghost town, thank God, as I've now got to do the walk of shame home on a Friday morning. It's only the odd taxi that passes me; I just keep my head down. My parents have left the door unlocked, so I open it as quietly as I can and start to sneak in.

I'm tiptoeing up the stairs when me ma shouts, "Is that you, Shelley?"

Shit, I've been sprung!

"Yes Ma."

"Where have you been?"

"Oh, I stayed at Cara's last night. We had a drink, and I fell asleep."

"Aye okay." That is all my Ma could say, but I think she knows otherwise.

I said I was at Cara's as my Ma and Da don't really know Cara's parents, they know them to say hello to but that's it. Where as if I had said Rochelle or Roisin, if she met their Ma's in the supermarket, she would have asked them, did I stay at their house. I don't know why I should be bothered as I'm almost twenty-one and an adult, but I guess you don't really want your mother or father to know their daughter was being a dirty stop out.

I go back to bed for a bit and set my alarm for ten thirty. Last night myself and Mattias agreed I would take him into Cork and show him the sites.

As soon as my alarm goes off, I jump straight out of bed and into the shower. I start getting myself ready and tie my hair back in a bun. I can't be bothered straightening it and doing all the palaver. That can wait 'till tonight, when we go out later. I put on my white jeans and a nice multicolored top with it. I can't decide: trainers or heels? Then think from a common sense approach. If I'm going to take Mattias to Blarney Castle, I'm best wearing trainers, so I pick my platform trainers. Although they are high, they are actually very comfortable.

I go downstairs and make myself some breakfast – cornflakes, and a cup of tea. The house is very quiet today. My mum comes through from the living room.

"Where is everyone?" I ask.

"Your Da's still at sea and your brother went out earlier to football. Your sister stayed at Liam's last night."

Liam is my big sister's boyfriend, they've been dating since they were like fifteen, high school sweethearts and they are both twenty-three now.

"Ah okay. Ma, can I borrow your car today? Only, I was wanting to go with a friend to Blarney."

She's heard me but by not giving me an answer, she wants to know more. Like 'who' the friend is.

"Oh, he's just someone I know."

"Tell me and I will give you the car," me Ma says with a laugh.

"Well, his name's Mattias, he's from Sweden."

"Sweden, aye. Oh, does he have blond hair, blue eyes and tan skin? Aye, take the car, but don't do what you did last time and bring it back with fresh air. You can put some fuel in it."

"Sorry ma, I will." I make a quick dash as she would have had me there all day asking lots of questions. Most folk must think the same as my Ma. The minute you mention Sweden – blonde hair, blue eyes, tan skinned. The ironic thing is he does in fact tick the box as your typical Swede if you want to call it that.

I tidy up my dishes and go upstairs and brush my teeth.

"Right, Ma, that's me away. I've got the car keys here," I shout up to her.

Just then my mum comes back through and gives me a cuddle.

"Watch yourself on them roads and take your time," she says sternly.

"Don't worry, Ma. I will."

Just as I'm closing the door she shouts after me, "I want to meet this Mattias."

"You will next Saturday, he's coming to the party," I say with a flash of a smile.

I start driving off to the staff accommodation, feeling excited at another day with Mattias. I pull up outside and shout up to his window, but he can't hear me, the windows are double glazed. I go back to the car and park the car properly. I walk up to the front door and buzz up. I wait a while until someone answers the intercom.

"Hi, I'm here to see Mattias, room six."

I can't hear what the other person says but I'm buzzed in straight away.

I walk up the short flight of stairs and get to Mattias' door.

I knock and shout, "Hello, Mattias it's Chelle."

The door opens and there he is looking gorgeous as usual. He is wearing a tight Levis t-shirt with blue jeans and he's carrying his jacket. As he stands before me, he looks so tall in front of me, I knew he was tall but didn't realize just how tall he was.

"Hello Chelle." He then leans in and kisses me.

I can feel my cheeks flushing again. Oh Christ, not this again, we won't get out the bloody door.

"Hi, how are you?"

"Good, so where are you taking me today.?"

"We're going to Blarney, then if we have time, into Cork," I say matter of fact.

We set off for Blarney, which is about thirty-five minutes in the car. I stop at the first petrol station and fill the car up, remembering what my mother said to me earlier. Once the car has a full tank of fuel, we are off, chatting along the way. Mattias is watching all the vast countryside as we drive along. I reach over to the left of me and put on the radio, the new Spice Girls song comes on – 'Viva Forever'.

"I love this song," I say while turning up the volume.

"I'm not really a Spice Girls fan, but I will listen to their music," Mattias says pulling a face.

As I'm driving along, I glance across to Mattias and I catch him looking at the radio, he's obviously listening to the words of their song. I then start singing along. Mattias looks over at me and smiles as the chorus comes on and we both start singing. We both turn to face each other and let out a laugh.

After the song finishes. Mattias asks, "Who is your favorite spice girl?"

"Erm, I actually like them all. They're all so different. I can't decide," I respond, trying to think.

"If you have to pick one, who would it be?" he persists.

"Geri or Victoria I think, nah wait – Mel B. Och I'm not sure. Geri?" I say still undecided.

My turn: "Who would you pick?" I ask, laughing.

Making a mental note to myself... this will be interesting to see which one he picks. Then I know what kind of woman he likes.

"The blonde one."

"My wee brother likes her also. She's called Emma – Baby Spice. Everyone has a favorite Spice Girl. My mum loves Sporty, my sister is Mel B," I proceed to tell Mattias. "When the Spice Girls first came out, me and my friends loved them. Like most of the universe we were and are all obsessed by them. That's when I started buying platform trainers and the dresses. Roisin had a few trackies like Mel C and Cara got her hair cut in a bob like Victoria."

"I can tell you really like them," he says with a grin.

We pull into the parking spot at the castle, and almost like clockwork, it starts to rain. We don't let that dampen our spirits. We head on up to admissions, which is a steep climb. I go to pay for the two of us, but Mattias won't let me.

"No Chelle, I will get this," he says seriously.

"No, it's fine."

"I insist," he says adamantly.

"Okay, thank you," I reply sincerely.

We start walking about the castle grounds. Mattias pulls out his disposable camera and clicks here and there. As we continue around the grounds, we read some of the plaques dotted about, telling us about the history behind the castle. We walk around and look at the magnificent gardens of the castle. As we follow the path into the castle on the second floor, where it's blocked off with an iron gate, we see murder hole. It was used when the castle walls were breached, and the enemy was running about inside. The hole was used by those defending the castle to pour boiling liquids on top of unsuspecting invaders. Further along we see a sign to the 'wishing steps'. It's said that if you can walk down and back up these steps with your eyes completely closed while making a wish, without stopping, your wish will come true within a year. Both Mattias and I follow the instructions and to my amazement we can both walk backwards, without falling. I make a wish, then Mattias. I shout over to him as he's slightly behind me. I make a wish to myself – to always be this happy as I am now in this moment.

"What did you wish for, Mattias?" I ask excitedly.

"If I tell you, it won't come true." He leans in and gives me a tender kiss on the forehead and puts his arm around me.

As we are walking away from the wishing steps, I keep thinking I wonder what he wished for. I wonder if he wished for him and I to always be together.

We start climbing up the next floor in the castle, all the way to the top and by the time we get there, we are both out of breath. Once we are at the top, the view doesn't disappoint. It is spectacular – you get a great view of the gardens from the top and just how vast and beautiful the gardens are. I take some photos at the top. Mattias takes one of me then I take one of him, and I ask a gentleman if he can take one of us both. We stand with our backs to the castle wall. Mattias puts his arm around me, and I lean into him and place my left hand over his tummy. Thankfully, the rain stopped a good five minutes beforehand and the sun is coming out from under the clouds.

We both say, "Cheeeese," and Mattias lets out a laugh.

The last stop is the famous Blarney Stone; we must lean backwards, hold on to an iron railing and then kiss the stone. According to folklore, once you've kissed the stone it bestows a gift of flattery and eloquence. Some say it was Jacob's pillow, brought to Ireland by the prophet Jeremiah.

After we leave the castle, I ask Mattias what he wants to do next.

"Do you want me to take you into the city of Cork?" I ask, trying to think of other places he might like to see.

"Yes, cool, thanks Chelle."

I park in one of the many car parks and then take a walk up the main street, holding hands and swinging them as we go. As we walk past the many shop windows in Cork, I have a nosy in most of them. Mattias waits for me as I have a rummage around the clothes stands. This is good, I think to myself, I thought most men hate shopping. He must be being polite I think to myself. I find a nice small coffee shop. We look in the window to read the menu, it looks just what we are after. We go in and order some food, I order macaroni cheese and a juice and Mattias orders the same.

"Thanks for today, I have enjoyed it. Ireland is a lovely place. I've truly fallen in love with the place and a girl." He stretches over and gives me a kiss.

"Oh no problem, I much preferred the company than looking at the castle, all by myself," I say with a smile.

I know the castle like the back of my bloody hand. My

mother and father were forever taking us on days out there when me and my siblings were wee.

"You will need to come sometime to Sweden, and I will show you all around," he says, reaching over to grab my hand.

"I bet you the weather is much better in Sweden at this time of year than it is here?"

"Yes, much better."

"Aye I thought so. We only get the sun for about a week a year here. That's why we all walk around like milk bottles. The only tan I get comes out of a bottle," I say sarcastically.

"Well, will you come some day?" he asks, staring at me now.

"Yes, maybe one day when I have money. I'm a poor student, now you know, Mattias." We both laugh.

My thoughts wander to what Mattias just said to me. I thought he just said that in general conversation to be nice, he must really want me to go to Sweden. Oh god I would love that. Jackie Kennedy, shades on living my best life. I smile to myself.

"What are you smiling at?"

"Just happy I've had a nice day, too," I explain.

After we have our food, we look in some more shops. We head back to the car and start the drive back to Cobh. I catch a quick glimpse of Mattias looking out of the window and he looks deep in thought.

"You look a million miles away. You alright?"

"Yes, I'm fine. I'm just thinking it's my older sister's birthday tomorrow, so I better stop by the pay phone before work and wish her a happy birthday. Or she will be angry with me."

"Remind me, what's her name again?"

"Annika. She will be twenty-five tomorrow," he says with a tender smile.

I get the impression they are close. I bet she's attractive, just like Mattias.

Chapter Seven

As we pull into Cobh, I ask Mattias if he wants me to drop him off at the staff accommodation, but he says no, he will get out at mine. He wants to walk down the hill and take in the view during the day.

Just as we are getting out of the car, I see my mum and sister coming out of the neighbor's house. *Oh fook*, I think to myself, if she sees Mattias it will be like the Spanish inquisition. My mother's eyes are squinting to see who is getting out of the car with me. She doesn't miss a trick, my mother. As Mattias turns around, I see my mother's jaw drop and she gives me a sly smile.

"Hello Chelle," ma shouts.

"Hi Ma, hi Shannon."

Now, I've both my mother and sister staring at me and Mattias. They start marching over to us.

"Well, Chelle, is this your friend from Sweden?" My Ma asks. "This is Mattias, he's from Stockholm."

"Hi," Shannon says with a smile and then turns to me and winks.

Mattias shakes both their hands and then gives them both a

kiss on the cheek. *Did I just see my mother blush?* I think to myself.

"Did you enjoy your day?" Ma asks.

Before I can answer, Mattias says, "Yes, we did thanks, Mrs. Doyle."

My mother lets out a roar. "Sure, now, you don't need to call me Mrs. Doyle. Call me Bridget. Come on in for a cuppa tea, Mattias."

My mum then proceeds to take Mattias by the arm and before he can protest, she's walking him up our garden path. Jesus poor Mattias, he doesn't know what he's let himself in for now, coming into the madhouse.

"Patrick, this is Mattias, he's Chelle's friend from Sweden," I hear my Ma say as I walk into my house and catch my Ma giving my Da a wink.

"Hello Mattias, nice to meet you."

My father has always been the quiet one out of the two of them, my mother has always been the hostess with the most-est.

"Sit down Mattias, take a seat, would you like a cuppa tea or a juice?" Ma asks.

"Sure, Bridget, the boy might want a beer," Da replies. "Do you want a beer, son?"

"Yes, great, why not."

My parents chat to Mattias for ages. I knew this would happen. Just then, my little brother comes in.

"Hello, you must be Kian."

"Hi," is all Kian can say.

My cheeky little brother, he's always so cocky and never lost for words. This is the first time I've seen the little shit speechless

"Would you stay for your tea Mattias, we are having lamb?" My mother asks. "Oh, thank you, but I don't want to trouble you."

"Sure, no bother, there's plenty to go round," My mother then proceeds to tell me to set the table for another person.

As we all sit down for dinner, I start to relax a bit. Kian seems to have taken to Mattias and the two of them sit talking about football. Mattias seems to know his football well and can follow everything my brother's saying about teams and players. My brother is football daft. There are six years between me and my little brother and just over two years between me and my older sister.

"So Mattias, I have to ask, are you an Abba fan?" my Ma asks.

"Yes, I like some of their music. They have done a lot for Sweden. You know, forty minutes outside Stockholm, Agnetha stays on an island there. I think she lives like a recluse now."

"Oh really, that's a shame. It was sad when they all split up. I love their music. Will you be coming to Chelle's party next Saturday? If you do, we'll be playing lots of Abba stuff," my mother says, laughing.

"Yes, I will definitely be there, I'm looking forward to it," Mattias says.

"Ma, I will oversee the music. You and aunty Orla will be limited to choosing songs."

"Yea, Ma your song choice is questionable," Shannon pipes up.

After dinner, I help my Ma and my sister tidy up and clean the dishes. My Da, Mattias and Kian sit chatting in the living room.

"He seems nice," Shannon comments, giving me her approval.

I can feel my cheeks blushing. "Yeah, thanks."

"Aye he's quite a fine man you've got there, Chelle," My mother says doing that annoying thing with her eyebrows, raising them up and down.

"Yeah, I like him, he seems nice. Ah guess we will see. He's only here for the season till the end of September and I'm back to uni in the middle of September. So, I guess we will see what happens."

I catch myself thinking about September and get the strangest saddest feeling in my stomach already at the thought of saying goodbye to him. I push the thought out of my mind as I don't want to start worrying about that and just enjoy the here and now.

After all the dishes are done, I go back through to the living room and just as I open the door, I can hear my Da, Mattias and Kian laughing. They all appear to be getting on well, which makes me happy.

"Do you wanna head down to yours now, Mattias?"

"Eh yeah, why not," he says and puts down his Guinness.

"Leave the man to finish his Guinness, Chelle," Me Da says.

"Oh, it's okay Patrick, I'm finished thanks and thank you for the lovely hospitality."

My Da stands up. "You're very welcome lad."

He puts out his hand and Mattias shakes it. Just then my mum and sister come back through, and he says his goodbye to them too.

He turns to Kian. "I enjoyed our chat about football, Kian. Hopefully I will see you again soon." He gives Kian a warm smile.

"Aye Mattias, you can come to the park and play football with me and ma pals if you want sometime."

"Thank you I might just do that," Mattias says sincerely.

Chapter Eight

On the way to Mattias', we stop at the local shop and buy two bottles of rosé wine. Once we arrive, I open the first bottle and pour us a drink. Mattias flips through his CDs, deciding what to play.

"Do you like Oasis, Chelle?"

"Yeah, I don't mind them."

Mattias proceeds to put on Oasis – 'Don't Look Back in Anger'. I sit on the windowsill with my glass of wine and think about the day I've had with Mattias, how he was just at ease meeting my family and all of them seemed to like him. I smile to myself. I feel happy, very happy at this moment.

"Now I know why you are so friendly, Chelle."

"Why?" I ask, intrigued.

"Because you have a lovely family. They all made me feel so welcome tonight. Your mum's funny and your dad seems like a nice man."

"Och they're alright I guess," I say with a laugh, but deep down, I know I have a wonderful family. "Ma little brother... he's an annoying little shit though."

"Aren't all brothers," he says with a tone of sarcasm.

Mattias comes closer and sits on the window beside me and starts to stroke my hair. I turn to face him and start to kiss him. The back of his hand gently strokes my cheek.

Mattias turns and looks me directly in the eyes and says, "You're beautiful, Chelle Doyle."

I can't muster up anything to say, so I smile up at him then rest my head on his chest. It suddenly dawns on me, Mattias knows my second name, but I've never asked him what his second name is.

"What's your surname?" I ask.

"Karlsson. I have a middle name also, Ludvig," he says proudly.

"That's a mouthful. Mattias Ludvig Karlsson."

"Do you have any middle names?"

"Yeah, Louise. Michelle Louise Doyle. My name sounds plain Jane boring compared to yours," I say with a grin.

I get up and head over to the CD player and have another scan through Mattias' collection.

"What are you putting on, Chelle?"

"Hmm I'm not sure, you have a lot to choose from."

I finally come to the decision: Puffy Daddy and Faith Evans – 'I'll Be Missing You'.

"Good choice," Mattias says, nodding approvingly.

"I like this song. I also like his song with Mase – you heard that one?"

"I don't think I know that one," Mattias replies.

He tops up my glass and then his own.

"That's the first bottle finished already! Are you trying to get me drunk, Mattias?"

"Of course not."

I giggle. "I'm only having the craic with you."

As I look out the window the sun is beginning to set. The

sky is lit up, beautiful colours of orange and purple across the skyline.

"Do you want to go down to the harbour for a walk and drink our other bottle down there, since it's a nice night?" I ask.

"Yeah, why not. Let me grab a jacket."

We head on down to the harbour and sit on one of the benches looking out to the Atlantic Ocean. I take two cups from Mattias' room and pour us another glass of wine.

"Cheers," I say clinking my cup against Mattias's cup.

"Cheers," Mattias leans forward and gives me a kiss.

We sit watching the sun going down, chatting and laughing while drinking our wine. I start to feel the alcohol take effect. Two strangers walk past and sit on the bench next to us. Mattias turns to talk to them.

"Beautiful sunset, isn't it?"

"Yes, lovely," the man says with an English accent.

I watch Mattias chat back and forth with the older couple and join in occasionally, but I sit back and observe how warm and friendly he is to people of all ages and from all walks of life. I've noticed this several times now with Mattias; he's at ease in anyone's company and always so warm and friendly. *He must be confident in his own skin*, I think to myself.

My teeth start chittering, I can feel how cold it's getting.

"Here, have my jacket."

Before I can protest, he takes his jacket off and wraps it round me.

"Thanks." I lean my head on his left shoulder.

We finish off the last bottle of wine. I start to stand up but start feeling slightly dizzy and have to sit back down for a second.

"I think I'm a bit merry."

Mattias is slightly giggly. "Yeah I think the wine and the sea air has gone to my head too."

He takes my hand, and we start walking round the harbour.

"Do you want to come back to mine?" Mattias asks with a smile.

"Alright," I say looking into his beautiful, blue eyes.

On the way round to Mattias' we see Roisin, Rochelle, Cara and Martin all trying to pile into the staff accommodation.

"Hey," I shout to them, stopping them in their tracks.

"What are you love birds up to tonight?" Rochelle shouts with a slur in her voice that makes me think she's had a drink also.

"Oh, we were down at the harbour having a drink."

"Oh, very romantic," Cara pipes in.

"What are you all up to tonight?" I ask.

"We've got a massive carry out here. We are going to Joanne's room for a party, there's a few more people coming, and a few are already up in Joanne's room," Roisin says.

Joanne is one of the Scottish live-in waitresses who is here for the summer season.

"Are you two gonna come up?" Rochelle asks.

"Yes, why not," Mattias says while nodding.

"Ah, but we don't have any drink left," I reply.

"That's okay. We have plenty," Martin holds up a carrier bag.

We catch up with the rest of them and start to follow them up the stairs.

"You all go in, I'm just going to get a shower first," Martin says.

As we are climbing the last set of steps to Joanne's room, I can hear 'Freed From Desire' playing and some laughter

"It sounds busy already," Cara says excitedly.

When we arrive, there are five people there already, all live-in staff from McLafferty's restaurant. There is Joanne, James the kitchen porter; he's a loud scouser, Mel another waitress from Dorset, Gerhard another one of the chefs who is German and Mark another kitchen porter from Scotland. All the live-in staff are more or less the same age as me, give or take a year or two and most of them are students except the chefs. Most just want to see a different place and make a bit of money for going back to Uni in the autumn.

Mark is quite an interesting character, he's from Stirling and is studying Zoology. He and Mattias seem to get on very well and are always chatting about different things.

"Pour yourself a drink folks," Joanne shouts over the music. She hands me a bottle of vodka in one hand and fresh orange in the other.

"Oh sure, thanks," I say.

I catch the back of Roisin; she is walking out the door. I suspect she's gone to see Martin in his room.

"Can I put on other music?" I ask while looking through the CD pile.

I come across the Dario G song Sunchyme which I love, and put this on. Within a few seconds of playing it, everyone is up dancing. We are all like sardines, jammed into Joanne's room. Mattias and Mark are waving their hands, Cara gets up on the window sill and is dancing away. Joanne is jumping up and down on the bed and we are all singing our heads off. Mattias sweeps me up onto his shoulders. Everybody is singing at the top of our lungs and waving our hands. Then, Mattias staggers back.

"Oh, shit, Mattias how much you had to drink? You're gonna feckin drop me," I giggle and trying to hold onto something for balance.

"Don't worry, I got you," Mattias then proceeds to sing Bob Marley's Don't Worry About a Thing.

James shouts, "Let's get this party started. I'm away to get my guitar back, in a minute."

Just then, Martin and Roisin come back in.

"We can hear you all upstairs singing," Martin pulls a funny face.

"We better tone it down a bit or Mrs. McLafferty will be giving us all our P45 in the morning," Rochelle says in a worried tone.

"Och fuck her. You only live once," Joanne says, matter of fact.

With Joanne not caring a hoot, that gives Cara the green light to turn the music up even louder and she starts singing and dancing. Me, Mark and Mattias start laughing at Cara and Joanne's carefree attitude.

"Cara you're blotto – you'll have a sore head in the morning," I say while catching her before she falls. James comes back with his guitar.

"Right turn the music off and tell me what you want! First up, I'm going to sing Oasis Wonderwall," James declares in his broad Scouse accent.

James starts tuning his guitar and then he's off, singing Wonderwall, and we all join in.

Mattias pulls me in close and we rock back and forth singing all the words. We start kissing and when we stop, everyone is looking at us as though they are singing the song to us. I turn my head away as I start to feel a bit self-conscious and embarrassed.

"Right, right I have a song for you James. Do you know Robbie Williams – Angels?" Cara asks while taking another stagger.

"Sit down, Cara, before you fall. I'll go get you a drink of water," Roisin says with a concerned expression on her face.

"Yeah, I know Angels." James starts strumming his guitar and singing the song perfectly.

"Oh, I love this song," Mark shouts.

We all join in again now that we are all slightly sozzled and the drink is flowing freely. I hate to think what we sound like, probably high-pitched hyenas or worse. I can feel my eyes closing together, I'm a bit drunk and tired. Mixing my drinks was definitely not a good idea, I tell myself.

Mattias looks over and brushes his finger softly above my eyebrow.

"Come on, let's get you home, you are tired and I'm drunk."

"Yeah, I think I need a glass of water. I feel sick," I say holding my stomach.

As we are leaving, another three staff are making their way into Joanne's room. Instinctively I just go to Mattias room, I can't be bothered walking all the way home, as I feel I could be sick at any point. I am twenty, after all. Mattias gets me a glass of water, I take a sip and lie back on the bed. Once my head is back on the pillow, I feel my head spinning.

"Oh, I've had way too much to drink tonight Mattias, I'm not drinking again, ever."

Just before I fall asleep, I ask Mattias what the time is.

"It's one thirty am," he replies with a gentle kiss on my forehead.

"Can you please set your alarm for half seven, as I need to be at work for ten am tomorrow."

Before I can hear his reply, I've crashed out like a light.

Chapter Nine

The next morning, I wake up to the alarm going off. I'm still on my left side the way I went to sleep the night before, with Mattias cuddled into me. Careful not to wake him, I wriggle out and hit the alarm off before getting a drink of water. My head is still sore so I lie back down for a few moments.

"Oh, Christ why did I mix my drinks last night," I say out loud. I'm going to be sweating in that restaurant today. I can see the seven-hour shift far enough, but I know needs must. Just then, Mattias starts to wake.

"Good morning," I say leaning down to give him a kiss.

"Good morning, Chelle. Isn't this nice? I could get used to this. Waking up with you every morning," he pulls me in close to his chest.

"Me too."

He cuddles me and I rest my head on his bare chest. He has the outline of a six pack and even his torso is very tanned. I run my fingers gently along his tummy.

He lets out a laugh. "That tickles."

I do it more to make him laugh. The more I do it, he grabs me and pins me down and starts tickling me.

"Ahaha, stop tickling me," I say, not really wanting him to stop.

"What time do you have to be in work for?"

"Nine am till noon, then back on five thirty 'till ten thirty."

"I better get ready and go, because I need to shower and get my work clothes. I start at ten so I will see you later."

I give Mattias a kiss. "See you soon."

He grabs me and pulls me back into bed.

"I'm not letting you go."

"I wish I could stay here all day, but I have to go see my parents. They will be wondering where I am."

After making my way from Mattias' back home, I can hear someone upstairs when I get into my house. I go into the kitchen and pour myself a big drink of juice to take up stairs with me, hoping it will cure my drouth. As I'm going up the stairs, my little brother is coming down.

"Morning Kian, what are you up so early for?"

"I've got a game today so I'm away to play football up north."

"Oh, that's an early start, good luck."

"Ta."

I go into my room and close the door before falling back and lying on my bed, being careful not to spill my juice. I check the time to see if I can lie in another wee while. *It's only ten past eight, so I'm going to lie in bed 'till eight thirty then get up and get ready for work*, I think to myself.

I end up early for work. I've got ten minutes before I start, so I pop into the kitchen and see Mattias. He's got his back to me, so I sneak up behind him. He is looking as hot as ever, polishing all the cutlery.

I put my hands over his eyes: "Boo."

He turns to me and laughs; he then leans over and gives me a kiss.

"Good morning, Chelle, how's your hangover?"

"Eh, I'm fine, thank you very much. Personally, I think it was all the singing and dancing."

We both laugh.

"Well, I just thought I would come in and say hello, before I start my shift."

He looks straight into my eyes, and I can feel myself blushing and getting hot and bothered already just from his gaze.

"You've cheered up my morning. Do you want to come round to mine when I finish tonight?"

"Yeah, will see you then."

We give each other another sneaky kiss before anyone comes into the kitchen and then I head off to start my shift with a spring in my step.

Once I'm downstairs, I go straight into the restaurant and, already, there are a few folks getting their breakfast. I see Cathy, one of the supervisors, running from the coffee station to the till looking quite harassed.

"Morning Michelle. Can you go and start collecting some of the dirty dishes, please? Joanne was supposed to be in at eight and she still hasn't appeared."

"Aye, no bother."

I then go and make a start. *Oh, Joanne must have had a late one last night if she slept in*, I think to myself. Once I've collected the dishes, I go and start wiping down the tables ready for the next lot of customers.

At ten thirty, Joanne finally walks in, looking the worse for wear. Christ, she looks how I feel today.

"Well, what time did you get to your bed last night after we left, was it a late one?" I ask quietly, making sure Cath doesn't hear me.

"Oh, Chelle, I don't even remember going to bed. I slept through my alarm and everything. Who's on today, are they raging with me?"

"It's Cathy; nah she didn't seem too bad."

Cathy sees Joanne and starts walking over to us.

"What time do you call this, Joanne?"

"Oh, I'm so sorry, Cathy. My alarm didn't go off and when I checked it, it needs a new battery."

"Aye, aye, usual excuse. Don't do that again. I was short-staffed this morning because Rochelle called in sick, she's been up all night with a sickness bug."

Both Joanne and I look at one another. Cathy then walks away to take an order.

"Some bloody sickness bug, her and Cara didn't leave mine till four this morning. They were singing going down the stairs," Joanne laughs.

"Christ, did many more people come after we left?" I ask.

"Nah, a few others popped in, but not for long. You should have seen my room this morning – bottles and glasses bloody everywhere. I couldn't even clean it up, I was too rough. Will need to do it when I go back after work."

"Oh god, the joys," I say feeling a bit sorry for Joanne. She jumps on the till to ring through a couple of coffees and breakfast for the people standing there. I go and collect more dishes.

Later in the day more staff start, and I finally get my break. I take my lunch and head on up to the staff room. I'm knackered and stretch my feet out on another chair while eating my lunch. I have a laugh to myself and think about Rochelle calling in sick. She must be so rough, even at uni when we would have wild nights out, she always made it the next day. I will need to give her a call, I think, when I finish work and hear all the chat about last night.

The day whizzes on and when I next look at the clock, I can't believe my luck, it's five minutes till my shift finishes. I've never been so happy to see five o'clock. The other supervisor Claire has taken over from Cathy for the late shift.

"Claire, that's five now. Is there anything else you'd like me to do before I go?" I ask.

"No, you get off Michelle, thanks," Claire says whole heartedly.

"See you tomorrow."

"Bye Michelle."

I run upstairs to get my jacket, and Joanne is sitting in the staff room having something to eat, as she slept in, she's got to work on a bit.

"Right, that's me off then, will see you later."

"Bye, Chelle. Might see you out later, I'm thinking about going to the pub with a few of the staff, for round two," she says with a laugh.

"Christ, you're keen, your hangover must have worn off now that you're raring to go again. I'm not sure if we are going out tonight, if we do will see you in Connelly, I'm sure," I say while grabbing my coat.

Chapter Ten

Today is my birthday. Twenty-one years ago, on the ninth of June, my Ma was in labour with me. I came into the world three days late and I think that's always been the case: running chasing my tail ever since. When I went downstairs this morning my Ma and Da had balloons and presents all set up for me. My Da came through with a hearty cooked Irish breakfast for me. Bacon, sausage, eggs, toast, black pudding, tomato, and my favorite white pudding and then to top it off, I had a Buck's fizz. I could get used to turning twenty-one every day. I couldn't move after breakfast, I sat on the couch like a beached whale and then finally, I remembered I had the hairdressers.

"Hello, Chelle, happy twenty first. Yer Ma told me," Siobhan says with a large grin on her face.

Siobhan is my hairdresser. She's about ten years older than me. I've been going to her since I was fourteen, my Ma and Shannon also go to Siobhan.

"You sit yourself down, honey," she pulls the chair out for me.

No sooner have I sat down than she's throwing the gown over me. Siobhan has a larger-than-life personality and like all hairdressers can get all the gossip out of you in five minutes, without even prying. Siobhan' happy go lucky personality is what really makes her likeable to most people. Her laugh is infectious and dirty, whenever she starts laughing, she makes others laugh too. Her laugh is usually funnier than the joke itself.

"So, what am I doing for Miss Michelle today, then?" she asks while looking at me in the mirror.

"Well, I'm hoping you've got time for this, but I would like some light blonde highlights in my hair, like a warm blonde, and then I would like you to give me an updo. Like big hair pinned up." I use my hands to express what I'm trying to say. The whole time I am talking and explaining, Siobhan is nodding and staring at me intently in the mirror, which can be a bit unnerving.

"Right, Miss, it's not every day you turn twenty-one: of course I will have time to do that. The only thing I will say with regards to the updo is that it sits a bit better if your hair hasn't been washed for a day, so we will see how we go. If it's a case of caking you with hairspray, then so be it. Tea or coffee lovely?"

"Can I just have a water, please?"

"Not a problem, coming up."

She comes back a while later with a glass of water and a load of magazines.

"Right, you have a read of them, and I will go make up your colour," she says.

I start to flick through *NOW Magazine* and read the latest celebrity gossip. I'm totally engrossed reading about all the latest on Geri leaving the Spice Girls. If it's not the Spice Girls on the cover, it's Kate, Meg, and Sadie the cool, wild Primrose Hill set – that's what the tabloids call them. All looking super class, even if they've been partying, falling out of super trendy night clubs, looking bleary eyed from one-to-many Margaritas. I wish I looked like that at the end of the night, I usually look like I've been pulled through a hedge backwards. I would love to be a fly on the wall at their parties. *A girl can only dream*, I tell myself.

"Right then, let's get this colour on you and get you looking a million dollars," Siobhan says.

"Cheers Siobhan. Am I not looking like a million dollars now?" I joke.

"You're looking good, girl – but when I'm finished with ya, you'll be ready for the red carpet."

We both start laughing but I'm more laughing at Siobhan's loud, dirty laugh. She sees me with the page of the magazine open on Geri's departure from the Spice Girls.

"Sure now, what did you make of that? Her leaving the band?"

"I can't believe she's left, Siobhan. You need all five of them to be the Spice Girls and Geri was a big personality. I hope they don't all quit now, too. I love them," I say sadly.

"Aye. She's getting too big for her boots and as you say they all need each other. I think she will regret it," Siobhan replies.

"Yeah, me too. I hope she comes back. Maybe she's just had a wobble as they are so famous, could you imagine being them, not even being able to go out and grab a pint of milk without someone recognising you," I say, feeling optimistic that Geri might come back one day.

"Hopefully, Chelle," Siobhan says while crossing her fingers at me in the mirror.

I watch her putting sections in my hair then putting the dye on and then sealing it with the tinfoil, she's very quick at it. She's perfected that to a fine art, from over the years of doing hair.

"So, Chelle, what's the plan of attack for the party tonight?" she asks.

"Well, I'm having a few friends and family around; my Ma is setting something up in the garden for us all. Fingers crossed it doesn't rain and then later will probably head to Connelly's," I explain, noting all the effort my family are going to right now to give me a night to remember.

"Och that sounds like a good night and what will the bell of the ball be wearing?" she says while nudging me on the arm.

"I've got this new dress, it's black and goes to just above my ankle. It's got spaghetti straps and above the bust it's black lace. Then I have high black leather heels, just to give me that extra bit of height," I say excitedly.

"Oh very fancy. I'm sure you'll be beautiful," she says with a sincere smile.

"Well now I'm having second thoughts; maybe I shouldn't have gone for all black. What do you think?" I ask Siobhan.

"I think if it's in your house, you'll be fine. But if you do go out to the pub later, maybe don't wear a black jacket – pick another colour."

Siobhan puts a few more foils in my hair and before I know it, she's got me under the heat lamp to sit for twenty minutes. Once she clears off, I put my head in another magazine. I have about five different ones to choose from and when I'm in the hairdressers I always look at the magazines for ideas on different hair updos. If I've got an idea in my head, I try my best to see if I can find a picture of it and find it easier to explain the style.

Once my hair is coloured and washed, Siobhan starts to blow dry my hair and appears to be in a world of her own, I can only think she is creating her magic.

"Right honey, remind me again, what you want done with your hair. You have great hair, it's so thick," she says, grabbing a section and holding it up for me to see in the mirror.

"As long as it's up high and you make it big, I don't care what you do."

"You sure you want me to pick?" Siobhan asks.

I give a nod in the mirror. She sections it all and then she starts looping it here, there and everywhere.

"Daa-rra," Siobhan grabs another mirror so I can see the back of my hair. I look into the mirror, and she turns it side to side. She pats the top of my hair: "The higher the hair, the closer you are to god," Siobhan says with her dirty laugh and a wink in the mirror to me.

"I really like it, Siobhan. It's lovely, thank you," I say sincerely.

It's like a big full bun, but loops in and out She's done everything I asked for – it's high and it's big, full hair that I love.

Once I leave the hairdressers, I start to make my way back home. Getting highlights and my hair styled has taken up half the day. I went in there at eleven am and it's now almost three pm. I start making a mental checklist in my head about what I've still to do before people start arriving at six thirty.

"Hey Ma, do you like my hair?"

"Turn around, Chelle. Sure, that's lovely, she's made a good job of it," my Ma says while touching the back of my hair.

"Chelle, you got not one, but two lots of flowers delivered for you while you were out. Aren't you a busy girl," my sister Shannon says with a grin.

I rush through to the living room and right enough there are two bouquets of flowers sitting there. The first one is in a basket with the most amazing floral arrangement, all pinks and creams. I open the small envelope that was attached to it and read what is written on the card.

"They are from Rochelle's Ma and Da. They are lovely – can I put them over there at the window?"

"Och that was nice of them both," my mother says while admiring the flowers.

I look at the next bouquet of flowers – they are a small bunch of red roses. I bet they are from Mattias, I think to myself, as you only really get red roses from your other half, and they look beautiful. I open the card to see who sent me these ones, which are stunning also.

To Chelle
All my love
Mattias xx

My face starts glowing red; the same colour as the roses. I have a bit of an audience now, as my family are all standing in front of me waiting patiently to hear who the roses are from.

"Well Chelle, are they from your Swedish hunk?" My sister asks.

I don't respond to my sister, as all four of them are having a chuckle so I just give a coy smile.

"Right, whose wanting fed before everyone arrives?" my mother asks.

"Och no Bridget, you've got a buffet there to feed the five hundred. We will all get something at the buffet," Me Da says.

"Ma, can I get a bowl of tattie soup with bread and butter," my wee brother asks.

I go up to my room and my clothes are all laid out already for tonight, just where I left them this morning. I pick some music; I fancy some dance music and decide on 'Music Sounds Better With You'. I press play on the CD player and lie back on my bed for a bit, making sure I don't squash my hair at the back and my neatly laid out clothes.

My mind drifts to Mattias. *He wrote "all my love" on his*

card. I ponder the thought. Does he really like me? He must if he wrote that, or maybe it's the language barrier, that's why he wrote it. My mind goes back and forth, wondering if he understood what he was writing.

I head in for a shower, ensuring I put a shower cap on so that my hair doesn't get wet after getting it done today. Afterwards I sit at my dresser in my room putting on my makeup. I'm not great at putting on makeup, not like Roisin – she's great at it, but I'm not rubbish either. I go with silver eye shadow, as I'm wearing silver jewelry. My aunty Orla, my Ma's sister, bought me a beautiful silver bracelet which I opened this morning. It has my gemstones throughout the bracelet for Gemini. Most people who are Gemini are said to have dual personalities, but I absolutely don't have that. I feel people get the same version of me all the time. Rochelle harps on all the time about star signs and what star signs are compatible and personality traits of people's star signs. Personally, I think it's a load of crap.

Once I'm already, I go down the stairs where my Da and Shannon are.

"There she is, the star of the show," ma Da says.

"You look lovely, Chelle."

"Thanks Shannon. Where's Ma?"

"She's in the kitchen, setting out the rest of the buffet."

Just then Shannon's boyfriend comes up the path.

"Shannon, there's Liam coming in."

"Oh, so it is," Shannon hurries away to see him.

"Right love, that's the buffet set up and I've got a load of chairs set on the patio in the garden. I hope I've got enough chairs! I borrowed some from Orla," my Ma, says sounding harassed.

"I'm sure there will be plenty, thanks Ma for everything," I stretch my arms out around her and give her a big cuddle. I appreciate all the effort she's gone too.

"Sure now, we couldn't let your twenty first pass without anything. Come on out and see it all set up," my Ma says, pulling my arm to follow her through.

Chapter Eleven

I head on through with my Ma and look at all the food she has laid out on the kitchen work tops. There is enough to feed a small army. I walk on some more through to the utility room at the back which leads to the garden. There is a load of plastic flute glasses all laid out on a big tray. Outside, there's fairy lights all hanging round and balloons everywhere. She has two tables set up with chairs on the patio and twenty-one banners all around. My dad is blowing up the last of the balloons.

"You alright there, Da? You look like you're gonna collapse."

"Yer Ma always gives me the best jobs, Chelle," he says, rolling his eyes.

"Oh, behave there, Patrick, you've sat on yer arse all day while I've been running around doing everything," my Ma replies.

Me and my Da look at one an other and laugh, while my Ma doesn't seem to see the funny side. She walks away with a face like thunder.

"She's out over there, aunty Orla," I can hear my wee brother say.

"Oh, there she is, the birthday girl herself. Come here and give your old auntie a cuddle."

"Hi aunty Orla, thanks very much to you and Uncle Paul for my present, it's lovely," I hold up my wrist.

"Did you like it, pet?"

"Yes, I love it, thanks so much."

"Hi uncle Paul, I was just saying to aunty Orla thanks very much for my present."

"No bother, Michelle. Are you having a nice day?"

"Yes, I am thanks."

"Good."

My uncle Paul walks over to my Da, who's now sitting on one of the chairs up at the top of the garden pouring a Guinness.

"Right Bridget. Let's get the music on. Shannon tells me Michelle has a Swedish friend, well put on some Abba later for him," my aunty Orla says, shouting over to my Ma.

"Oh aye, wait till you see him Orla," my Ma gives an approving nod.

My mum then does as she's told by her younger sister and puts on Abba's Dancing Queen. More of my family have arrived now, a few of my Da's siblings and their family. My mum only has the one sister, whereas my Da has two brothers and a sister, and I have loads of cousins. However, out of all my aunts and uncles I'm closest to my aunty Orla and uncle Paul. My aunty Orla doesn't act her age, she still thinks she's young and trendy, she's more like one of my best friends than an aunty and there isn't anything I wouldn't tell her.

There is loads of noise at the house now with the music and people talking loudly over the music, however in the distance I can hear Mattias' voice.

"We have good summers in Stockholm, but in the winter, it gets very cold."

I interrupt Mattias talking to my Aunty Janice – my Da's sister and her husband Ted.

"Hey, you got finished early?"

"Yes, I asked Jacob to let me finish early today. I didn't want to be late for your party," he says with a sincere smile.

Mattias then reaches in and gives me a kiss and a cuddle. I get a bit shy only because I'm conscious all my family's eyes are on us.

"Thank you for my flowers, they are lovely." I take him by the hand upstairs to my room to show him where I put my flowers, pride of place on my bedroom windowsill.

"I'm glad you like them. I have another surprise for you also," he says with a glint in his eyes.

He sits down on my bed. Oh, Christ is he gonna propose to me? *Calm down, Michelle, you bloody wish*, I think to myself. He motions me to sit down beside him and hands me a small box – it looks like a jewelry box. I open it and find a beautiful gold necklace with a gold heart hanging from it and in the centre is a tiny diamond.

"Oh, that's beautiful, Mattias, thank you so much. I love it. You shouldn't have bought me all this, that looks awfully expensive."

I am worried, knowing McLafferty's doesn't pay mega bucks, and I don't want him spending all his hard-earned cash on me.

"It's fine. I wanted to get you something nice," he says sternly.

He then takes it out of its box and starts to put it around my neck. I go to the mirror in my room and have a look at it.

"I really like it. Thank you," I say honestly.

He's standing behind me watching me in the mirror and I turn round and give him a cuddle and start kissing him.

"Don't do that to me Chelle, or we won't get out of your bedroom," he laughs.

"What if I don't want to leave my room and just stay up here with you all night?"

"I think your family would have something to say about that. They're all here to celebrate your birthday."

"Hmm I suppose."

We start to kiss once more. He pulls away from me and looks into my eyes, all I can see staring back at me are the bluest of eyes.

"I love you Chelle. Come; let's go and celebrate your birthday."

As I walk down the stairs, I feel like I am walking on cloud nine. *What the hell, he just said the "L" word*, I think to myself. My belly is doing somersaults and all the hairs on my arms are standing up. I feel like I must pinch myself, did I really hear right.

"There you are. Bridget, I've found the love birds. What were you pair doing up the stairs?" My aunty Orla asks, giving us both a wink.

Mattias smiles shyly. I don't think he knows yet just how to take my aunty Orla.

My Da is going through his CD collection. Christ, I hope my Ma doesn't let him loose. My Da's choice of music is questionable.

"Here Da, let me pick something, please, it's my party."

"Sure, but none of your boom, boom crap."

I have a look through the CD's and think, right let's get this party jumping. I pick out The Tamperer featuring Maya – Feel it. Right, that should get everyone up.

"Chelle, what you wanting to drink?" My Ma asks.

"Can I please have a vodka and coke?"

I head out to where all my friends are. Mattias is up there already chatting to Rochelle and Roisin.

Martin and Joanne stand up to greet me. "Happy birthday, Chelle, and here's a wee something for you."

Martin then gives me a hug and Joanne hands me a small gift bag.

"Thanks folks."

"You look nice, Chelle," Cara says and then twirls me round to look at the back of my hair.

"I like your shoes, Cara, they are nice. Did you get them from Shelly's shoe shop?" I ask.

"Yes, as soon as I saw them, I thought I'm having them. Definitely Spice Girl shoes."

"I looked at them, but they didn't have them in my size. They were out of stock," I say, still feeling disappointed.

I can hear singing in the background. Well, if that's what I want to call it and look around. There's my aunty Orla on the karaoke singing her heart out to Celine Dion – All By Myself.

"Oh, dear good, that's wild. She sounds like she's being strangled," I say to the group.

Cara, Rochelle and Roisin all like my aunty Orla and have a good laugh with her. They start egging her on by clapping and shouting. The song is soon over and everyone starts laughing.

"Right, come on, who's going to come up here next. I've just made a fool of myself, it's someone else's turn," Orla shouts.

Just then Rochelle shouts out, "Right get the birthday girl up and give us a song."

"Oh god no, the vodka hasn't kicked in yet. Someone else go up, please."

Mattias grabs me by the hand and pulls me to the patio where the karaoke is.

"Come on Chelle, it will be a good laugh, we will sing together."

"Hmm I'm not sure. I'm a terrible singer."

"Come on, it will be fun. I will pick a funny song for us both to sing," he says confidently.

"Okay then, let's give it a bash."

After Mattias' reassurance and persuasion, he has me up on the patio ready to sing. I've never been one that's full of confidence and outgoing, even at school. I just like to blend in and fade into the background. I'm not unconfident either, but I'm not right out there in your face. Whereas Mattias is at ease with people and people seem to warm to him and he appears to never take himself too seriously.

"Right, you ready, Chelle?"

I give a nod and then he sets it up. I'm watching the screen, my heart beating, wondering what the hell he has chosen for us. The words start to appear on the screen.

"Hiya Barbie..."

After the first few lines, I'm starting to get into the rhythm of it and letting my guard down. Mattias' confidence is flowing. We are singing the lyrics to one another, leaning forward to each other laughing and singing. Like there is no one else in the room, just the two of us. At the end of the song my Ma is the first to start clapping and cheering then everyone else joins in. Mattias laughs and lifts my arm up in the air.

"Happy Birthday to my Barbie," Mattias shouts over the mic.

Oh, hell, I feel mortified now. I look over at my friends and I don't need to say a word to them, only eye contact. They know I'm embarrassed, I don't want to look over at my parents as my Da is quite straight laced. That's the beauty of having good friends that know you so well, you don't need to exchange any words, just some body language and instantly they know exactly how you're feeling. My aunty Orla has just taken over organising the karaoke and no one is safe when she's around.

"Right Patrick, get yer arse up here and give us all a song."

"Oh, Christ no, Orla, I don't think anyone's wanting to hear me sing."

Everyone then starts telling my Da to get up and eventually he bows to peer pressure.

"Okay, okay I'm gonna sing Rod Stewart – We Are Sailing."

Mattias turns to me, "Your dad is actually not a bad singer."

"Aye I'm thinking that myself. I didn't know he had it in him," I say proudly.

"On yer self Da. Ma is that how you met? Did Da charm you with his singing voice?" my sister Shannon shouts.

Everyone is all dotted about the garden, and the patio. There's a few folks that's in the house that are now coming outside also. Behind them I see my Ma and sister walking with my birthday cake. It's a chocolate cake in the shape of the number twenty-one.

I lean over to blow out my candles.

"Wait, Patrick, go get the camera," my mother asks.

"I hope you made a wish," my aunty Orla shouts out.

When I bend over to blow out the candles, I catch my mum looking at my chain. She's now holding it in one hand, while holding the cake in her other, getting a better look of it.

"That's lovely Chelle, who got you that?" she asks.

"Mattias. He gave me it earlier tonight."

"It's lovely Chelle, but you know the old saying silver and gold should never be seen."

She's referring to the fact that my earrings and bracelet are both silver and my chain is gold.

"Ah know ma. I already had my jewellery on earlier when he gave it to me, and I just put that on also. I thought it was pretty."

"It sure is pretty, love," ma Ma says not taking her eyes off the chain.

Now there's a small gathering looking at the necklace.

"That's lovely Chelle. Mattias, you've got good taste," my aunty Orla says.

My Da comes running back through with the camera and takes a photo of me standing near the cake. My uncle Paul takes one of me, Ma, Da, Shannon and Kian. The last photo is of me and my friends and Mattias is standing right at the back due to him being so tall.

My mum starts dishing out the cake and after some of my family have had a slice, a lot of them start saying their goodbyes and leaving. Not my aunty Orla though, she's just getting warmed up and she's pulled my poor uncle Paul up to dance. The drink is flowing, and everyone appears in good spirits. I'm not sure if it's the alcohol or they're just enjoying themselves. My wee brother has a few of his pals over at the party. I catch the three of them sneaking down the stairs and pinching three cans of beer in the kitchen when they think no one is looking.

"Caught! I'm gonna tell Ma."

"Och, Chelle please don't. We're only wanting to see what it tastes like," my brother strops.

"Right, if I catch you sneaking any more, I'm telling Ma," I say sternly.

The three of them run back up the stairs with their beer.

I head back out to the patio and can hear laughing, Mattias is sitting laughing with my Ma, Da, aunty, uncle, sister and Liam. I hang back just at the outside door and watch him. I watch all their body language the way they interact with Mattias and can tell they all like him. He's the centre of the conversation and they are all hanging on to his every word. I get why people like him – he's warm, friendly, and straight forward with no hidden agendas. I pour myself a drink and head back out to join them.

"Right Chelle, since it's your birthday, let's all of us sing on the karaoke," Roisin says.

"What will we sing?"

"Let's sing 'Stop' by the Spice Girls," Rochelle says.

We all get up onto the patio, me, Roisin, Cara and Rochelle.

I turn to Rochelle. "We need another person." Cara goes and pulls Shannon up. She loves the Spice Girls too.

My sister comes up to the patio to join us, she doesn't need to be asked twice. She's quite merry all the white wine she's been throwing back. The five of us all get ready to start singing and I'm up first.

After the first verse, I pass the mic along; my aunt and my mum are up dancing in the garden. When the song finishes everyone is clapping and laughing. I check my clock in the kitchen. I wonder if we should go to Connelly's for last orders.

"Girls, it's eleven thirty, are you wanting to go to Connelly's or stay here?"

"I don't mind, Chelle, you're the birthday girl," Cara says.

The others nod in agreement with Cara.

"Okay, well, since I'm the birthday girl, I say let's go down to Connelly's for a boogie."

We all drink up and say our goodbyes to my family and to my surprise my sister and Liam join us too. We all walk down the hill and around the bay to the pub laughing, singing, and dancing as we go down the road.

Chapter Twelve

"Well, good morning, sleeping beauty," Mattias says, standing at the bottom of the bed with two plates.

"Good morning," I say giving a stretch and then sitting up to see what Mattias has cooked.

It's toast with a poached egg. "That looks nice, I guess you've been a busy bee this morning."

"You were fast asleep. You didn't move when I got out of bed."

"Yeah, I was so tired last night with all the extra shifts I've been doing. I need to get the extra pennies in for starting back at uni."

All I seem to have done this summer is party and spend money I think to myself, and the months have just flown by. I better get my finger out and start saving. One minute I was doing my exams in May and then the next I met Mattias. Before I knew it, the first of September was already here. I've had the best summer ever, but like all good things it's now coming to an end, and it worries me. I go back to uni in two weeks, Mattias is going to come and stay with me and Rochelle in the flat for a week and fly back home, but after that, I don't know if I will ever see him again and even thinking about it makes me sad. I've fallen head over heels for Mattias and the thought of never seeing him again leaves me quite depressed inside.

"What is it? You look a million miles away, Chelle."

"Och nothing. I'm just thinking that's all."

"Thinking about what?"

"What I'm going to do when you leave and go back home to Stockholm," I say sadly.

Suddenly Mattias' face changes from a serious expression to a sad one. "You can come visit me. My family would love you. I will come and visit you all the time and next year I will hopefully come back and work again for the season."

"Yes, I know," I lean my head on his shoulder.

I start getting tucked into my poached eggs and toast before they get cold. I choose to start living in the here and now and stop thinking about the end of September and just enjoy my time left with Mattias.

"This is good, thanks,"

"That communal kitchen in there is disgusting. I had to clean all the pots in the sink before I could start cooking," he says repulsed.

"I've never been in there, but surely it can't be the staff. Maybe it's the backpackers who rent the other rooms," I say.

"Who knows. I just wish people would clean up after themselves," he says with an annoyed tone to his voice.

"Do you fancy going into Dublin today and I can get the car off me Ma and Da. We could see what's on at the pictures?" I ask.

"Yes, that would be nice," he smiles.

"Okay. I will head up the road shortly and get organised. You can either come up with me or pop up later?"

"I will come round later if that's okay. I'm going to tidy up in here and then call my parents back home in Sweden. I will need to go to the shop to get change."

"Okay," I say before reaching over and putting my plate and Mattias' plate down on the ground then snuggling back in beside him. He pulls me in tight and I stretch out over his chest. With his left hand, he tilts my chin up to kiss me as our mouths meet at the same time.

"You're driving me crazy, Chelle."

"I like driving you crazy," I say, letting out a naughty giggle.

After our morning aerobics, I make a mental note to myself. I really need to get out of this bed or we are going to end up in it all day. The last couple of months, there's not been much sleep going on in this bed.

"What are you giggling at?"

"I'm thinking I really need to get out of this bed at a reasonable time today. Or we will end up staying here all day."

"Is that a bad thing?" He says suggestively.

"No, but I'm thinking if I can get to Dublin at a good time, I can go buy a few things for uni."

I find somewhere eventually to park in Dublin. It's Friday lunchtime and I think everyone has the same idea.

Once we park up, we walk for a bit and then come onto the shopping district and decide to look around a few shops. Mattias stops at a couple of sports shops and tries several pairs of trainers on.

"What do you think of these, Chelle?"

"Yeah they are nice, but I liked the other ones better."

He then looks in the mirror, deciding which ones to pick.

"I think I will get these," he says lifting the trainers with the blue tick.

"Good choice."

We stop at a few souvenir shops in Dublin. Mattias wants to buy some stuff for his family back home. He picks up a few Irish leprechauns, as I told him the story a while ago surrounding the Irish folklore myth. Once he's had a look round, I see the shop I want to go to for stationary.

"There's International, I will be five minutes. I'm just going to nip in there."

"Okay. I will wait outside for you."

I can never walk past International without going in and having a look around. I don't think any girl can. You can always find something in this shop. Sure enough, I've found khaki combat trousers and a nice three-quarter length tight top, all for the great price of thirty quid! Great, I think to myself, another bargain.

"Do you want to head on over to see what's on at the pictures now, Mattias?"

"Yeah, sure."

When we get to the cinema, there isn't too much to choose from. *As Good as it Gets* with Jack Nicholson, *Ever After* featuring Drew Barrymore or *The Parent Trap.*

"What do you fancy watching?" I ask.

"I like all Jack Nicholson's movies," He states.

"Yeah me too. He's great. Have you ever seen *The Shining*?" I ask.

Mattias then impersonates, "Heeeere's Johnny!"

We both burst out laughing. We patiently wait in the queue to pay, and I start thinking maybe we should have gone to see *Ever After*. Drew Barrymore is an excellent actress also, and I would have liked to see the film but didn't want to seem too girly. Mattias buys the tickets and won't take money off me for my ticket. I pull money out my purse and go to offer to pay my share, but he's adamant he wants to pay.

"Please, just take this," I protest.

"No. It's fine."

It's our turn at the sweet counter and the woman behind the counter is staring at us. "Okay, let me buy the sweets then,"

He shakes his head in annoyance and laughs. "Okay, okay, you get the sweets."

"Do you want sweet popcorn or toffee?" I ask.

"I don't mind, you pick."

"Can I please have a large toffee popcorn, a Coke and a Fanta please."

The lady goes to the juice dispenser and starts processing our order. Once we get our sweets, we go through the other set of doors to get our seats. The lights are slightly dimmed and it's a bit hard trying to find our seats. We eventually find them; they are up the back at the start of the aisle, which is good because if I need the toilet, I hate squeezing past people and saying excuse me.

Just as I'm settled in ready to watch the film, someone comes and sits in front of me and it's always the same. A tall person, which means you've got to move about so that you can see the picture, because if you don't all you will see is the back of a head.

The film is just about to start now. While the adverts were on, we eat most of the popcorn. I feel a bit sick. I hand it to Mattias so that I'm not tempted again, and he puts it on the floor. We both snuggle into each other to watch the film, Mattias puts his arm around me, and I lean onto his shoulder.

Chapter Thirteen

Today's the day that I'm saying bye to my family and making the long journey back to Belfast in time to start uni. My Da's driving me and Rochelle back up to Belfast. I know I'm only in Belfast, but I will miss my family when I go back to uni. Even my Ma's cooking and the noise in the house and it pains me to admit it, even my annoying little brother. I miss all four of them when I go away for long periods. In the last few years, my older sister and I have gotten close. When we were younger, all we did was argue and she did what most big sisters do (tease their younger siblings) but I will miss them all.

Mattias is coming up to see me before I head off and to say bye, even though he will see me again in two weeks' time when he finishes McLafferty's for the season. He wants to see my family as well just in case he doesn't see them before he leaves Cobh. My mother said she wished he stayed nearer as she sees how much we both like each other.

"Chelle, that's the car all cleared out for you and Rochelle's stuff, if you want to start bringing it down," me Da shouts.

I start taking my first case down the stairs. I go out the front door down the drive to where my father's waiting with the car open. The weather is grey, wet, and miserable today, matching my mood.

"Here, Da, I'm just going in to get some more of my stuff," I say.

"Aye okay, Michelle," me Da says and starts lifting the case into the boot.

Just as I turn to walk back up my drive to get the rest of my stuff, there he is bounding along the road: my sexy Scandinavian. Right on cue.

"Hey, how's it going. You're right on time," I say with a smile.

"I'm always punctual, Chelle," he says flashing me his trademark smile.

"Hello Mattias. How are you? Terrible bloody weather today, isn't it?" my father shouts at him.

"Yes, although I'm getting used to this weather in Ireland now."

I leave my Da and Mattias talking and walk back inside to get more of my stuff. I come back out with another two cases, and I can tell by my Da's face he's not too pleased.

"Michelle, remember I've got to get Rochelle's stuff in the car as well," he snaps at me.

"I know, Da. That's it all. Mattias, come with me a minute."

Mattias follows me into the house and upstairs to my room. "I have a surprise for you. Close your eyes. I remembered you telling me you like surprises so close them and no peeking, Mattias."

He closes his eyes. I then go into one of my bedroom drawers and pull out a small box. I turn around to make sure he's still got his eyes closed.

"Okay, open them." I hand him the box.

He opens it and looks surprised when he sees inside. It's a a gold St. Christopher chain and had the initials MD & MK 1998 engraved on the back of it.

"That is beautiful Michelle. Thank you." Mattias kisses me.

"Turn it over to see the back of it. I got our initials engraved on it," I say proudly.

He stands up, then, picks me up off the ground and kisses me hard on the lips.

"Thank you, Chelle. You'll always have my heart."

"And you mine," I say gently.

We embrace each other once more and I get the feeling he feels quite sad also, knowing we don't have long until we are both worlds apart and our time together joined at the hip will soon be over. It's a thought that keeps creeping into my mind and the more I try and push it away, the more it keeps coming back. I know we both say we will keep in touch and that he will come back next year to work, but it's a long time till next year and we will be thousands of miles away from each other and a lot can happen in that time.

He gives me one last gentle squeeze and a kiss. "I love you, Chelle."

"I love you too."

I've had a few boyfriends before, but I would say Mattias is my first love and they say you never forget your first love and here in this moment, I don't think I will ever forget this gorgeous man standing in front of me.

We go back outside to the car, and I give my brother, sister, mum and Mattias a cuddle.

"You watch yourself in Belfast," me Ma says.

"I will Ma. Once Mattias goes back to Sweden, I will come back every second weekend."

"Chelle, I will come up and see you in November. I've

asked for holidays at the office and will stay for a week to start my Christmas shopping," my sister Shannon says.

"Sure, no problem, Shannon. Right, I better be off then, Rochelle will be waiting on us." I lean in and kiss Mattias again.

"See you in two weeks, Michelle," he says while stroking my face.

As I jump in the car the four of them are standing waving me and me Da off, until we are around the corner and can no longer see them. We stop off at Rochelle' and her parents are waiting on us. She's all packed up and ready to go. My Da makes general chit chat while putting Rochelle's cases in the car with her parents. Rochelle climbs in once my Da has loaded everything in, we wave bye to them as we drive away.

"Da can I put on the radio?"

"Aye. As long as it's not too loud."

I stick on the radio, hoping for an upbeat song to lift my mood, it's anything but. Billie Myers – 'Kiss the Rain'. My gran once told me a saying and it's always stuck with me and now all I can think about is her saying: when you're happy you enjoy the music, but when you're sad you understand the lyrics. This song is going to depress me even more, I think to myself and then reach back over and turn the radio off. My dad gives me a glancing look, as if to say, *I thought you wanted the radio on*, but instead says nothing and puts his eyes back firmly on the road ahead. I just sit and stare out the window at the passing countryside, with my own thoughts, forgetting I've got Rochelle for company. The weather is starting to clear up a bit now the further north we drive and a rainbow appears. Rochelle and I chat a bit back and forth, although I suspect she can tell I'm not much up for talking today. I'm more consumed by my own thoughts and feelings. We pull over and get a quick toilet stop and my Da stretches his legs, then back on the road again to Belfast.

Just a little after six pm we arrive at what's going to be our new home for the next year while we are both at Uni. We pull into Lisburn Road and my Da gets as close as possible to the flat. It's above a shop and not far from the uni, which is great. Our last flat was a bit out of the way, we didn't like it very much and both made a pact that we would get a new flat for our second year. We have our own door; we walk in through the porch and then there are some stairs going up to our flat. The living area is open and airy, the kitchen goes off the living area, it's like a living room come diner. Both bedrooms are similar in size and the bathroom has a bath and separate shower. My Da makes sure we are both settled in and bids us farewell, then heads off back on the four hour plus round journey back to Cobh.

"I'm knackered, Chelle. Do you want to get a takeaway, and we can go get a shopping in the morning?"

"Aye sounds good. I will unpack and sort everything tomorrow. I'm just going to make up my bed and then I will walk round to the takeaway with you."

The first night in our new flat goes well. Once we make up our beds, we are so tired that we go straight to sleep. I get up early and start unpacking all my stuff. I don't need to be officially back in uni until Thursday so that gives me a few days to get myself organised and sorted. I've not heard any noise coming from Rochelle's room this morning so I've been conscious to tip toe round and not wake her, she must be needing her beauty sleep.

Once I have all my stuff in order, I make my bed then throw open the curtains. It looks like it's going to be a nice day in Belfast today. I might go for a walk to one of the museums and get some food shopping on the way back. I like to be out and about when the weather is nice. I think it's an Irish thing because we don't get great weather at the best of times, I always feel when it's a nice day to make the most of it. My Ma would always tell us that or have me and my siblings doing something when we were younger, so we weren't cooped up in the house.

I hear Rochelle's door opening and shout through to her, to see if she wants to do something later together. I then pad through to the kitchen on my bare feet and go to make myself something for breakfast then realise there is no food in, so instead make do with a cup of tea.

Later, once Rochelle had put all her stuff away and we both had a wash to freshen up, we decided on going to the Botanic Gardens in Belfast. First though we go straight to a cafe and get some lunch.

"What are you fancying today, Rochelle?"

"I think I will get a soup and sandwiches."

I decide on this also and get a portion of chips for the two of us to share. We are both starving by the time our food is delivered to our table.

"Hmm this is good Chelle," Rochelle says keeping her eyes firmly placed on her scotch broth soup.

"Yes, just what the doctor ordered."

We finish all our food leaving nothing for the waiter to take away and then set off to the Botanic Gardens now that our tummies are full. We walk for a good twenty minutes until we are finally there. I'm enjoying the walk as the sun is peeking through the clouds and there isn't a bit of wind in sight, it feels warmer than what it is for a September day. I'm also enjoying walking off our lunch. You would think we hadn't eaten in a week with how quickly we scoffed our food down.

I can start to see the large dome on top of the gardens as we get closer. We read the map of the gardens and a bit about them. We then start following the signs and the people in front of us. The gardens were built in eighteen twenty-eight, later in eighteen fifty-two the dome was added and has been a feature of Belfast ever since. It was made from curved iron and glass. As we wander around the gardens, they are very impressive: both Rochelle and I comment on that. All the plant collection is from the southern hemisphere. We chat back and forth about starting back at university and looking forward to seeing all our friends we made last year and to hear their tales of what they got up to in the summer.

"Wait till we tell Aoife that you have a Swedish boyfriend now, Chelle. I wonder what she will say to that," Rochelle says.

We both look at each other and laugh. We don't need to say anymore as we both think the same about her. Aoife will have plenty of questions for me. She's nice but probably the nosiest person I have ever met. She can also be quite judgmental about people at times, almost like a grand seniority complex which I've always been surprised about. Especially when she talks about her life and family, I don't think she had the easiest of times. Instead of showing people compassion and understanding she judges and a few times last year, I could feel her get under my skin and had to say it to her. Her nosiness doesn't bother me, I find it funny.

After we see the gardens, we sit chatting on one of the park's benches and we both agreed we needed to go and get some food in. Rochelle wants to call a taxi to take us to the supermarket, I then protest and tell her the walk will do us both good and remind her she is only twenty-one – not fifty-one. We agree if she walks to the supermarket, we will get a taxi back home with all the food.

Chapter Fourteen

Today is the day Mattias is coming to see me and stay with me for a week before he heads back home to Sweden. I just had a uni lecture in the morning so now I'm rushing home to make sure the house is tidy for him arriving. He's getting the bus up and is hoping to be here for the back of four, and from the bus he will just get a taxi to the flat. I stop in at the local supermarket and get some food. I'm going to cook tonight for me, Mattias and Rochelle. I can't decide yet what to cook so I have a look round the aisles in the supermarket looking for inspiration. I finally choose spaghetti bolognese and garlic bread. *You can't go wrong with that*, I think.

I keep checking the window to see if there is any sign of Mattias yet, it's half four and he's still not here. I've cleaned the flat and got dinner already. It's just a case of heating it up and putting the bread in the oven. I picked up a bottle of red to have with it. The washing has now finished and I'm in the middle of hanging it up when I hear a knock at the door. *Yes*, I think to myself, *he's here!* and run down the stairs as fast as I can. I leave the remaining washing thrown on a heap in the middle of the floor.

"Hello you," I say, then spring forward, bounding into his arms.

"Hello Chelle, I've missed you."

He gives me a flash of his smile, all pearly whites. He leans forward, and our eyes meet, we start kissing as though we haven't seen each other in years. My hands move up to his face and I cup either side of his face. He has one hand on my back and the other is starting to travel down to my bottom. We kiss for what seems like an eternity and we must be drawing attention, as we hear a car beep, which brings us back to our senses. All Mattias' bags are still lying outside the door. We step back out and bring all his bags in. I put his cases in my bedroom and then I give him a grand tour of our flat. Mattias goes to the window to look at the view, not that there is much, it looks on to a busy main road. I go up behind him and cuddle him leaning my head on to his back. Mattias turns round and we start kissing again, just then I hear the door close and footsteps coming up the stairs.

"That will be Rochelle," I say as I walk to the living room door.

"Hello Rochelle, nice to see you," Mattias gives her a cuddle and a kiss on the cheek.

"Hey, Mattias nice to see you too," Rochelle says warmly.

"I've made dinner for the three of us."

"You didn't have to make any for me. I feel like a gooseberry, I don't want to cramp your style," Rochelle laughs.

"Don't be daft. I've made it now, so you better eat it," I say teasingly.

"Och, okay then. Later I've organised to go with a few of the folks from uni to a couple of bars to give you two love birds some space."

"You don't need to do that," I say feeling a bit bad.

"Nah, you're fine. I'm wanting to go out for a few tonight to see if there's any craic."

I go over to the oven and heat it up for the garlic bread. I then set up the table while Mattias and Rochelle talk about all the gossip from McLafferty's leaving party for all the summer staff. I pour the three of us a glass of red wine and then take Rochelle and Mattias glasses over to them.

"Sláinte, Chelle," Rochelle says.

"Thank you," Mattias says while giving me a warm smile.

The garlic bread is cooked in no time, and I start serving up our dinner.

"This looks good," Mattias leans into me looking quite surprised and giving it a once over.

"Sure, you haven't tried it yet. Wait till you've tried it," I say giggling.

When we are all finished Mattias, being the true gent, gathers our plates and starts clearing up.

"Just leave them and I will do them," Rochelle shouts over.

"You're fine, we will get them," I say and then get up to give Mattias a helping hand.

A while later Rochelle says her goodbyes before leaving. Mattias and I then snuggle down on the couch to watch some TV. I flick through the channels but the telly's crap. I've got my feet over Mattias's legs, he takes off my socks and starts tickling my feet.

"Don't, stop it, that's too tickly!" I say giggling but not really wanting him to stop.

This is Mattias' last night with me before the day I've been dreading for the last few months arrives and he flies back home to Stockholm. I feel very sad the more I think about him leaving. I could get used to him staying with me, the days that I've been going to uni, he's been walking about Belfast taking in the local sites then coming back home and cooking for me and Rochelle. Tonight, he has cooked Swedish meatballs for us to try. Rochelle has been calling it the last supper and trying to lighten the mood for Mattias and I, both of us can only muster a smile.

"They look nice," both me and Rochelle say.

I cut into one of the meatballs and put it in my mouth. I must admit I wasn't so sure to start with, but because he had gone to the effort, I thought it would be rude if I didn't try them. When I chew into the meatball, I'm pleasantly surprised. *Looks can be deceiving*, I think to myself, *that was nice.* After dinner we put on a video. Rochelle and I stopped at Blockbusters on the way home and picked a film for the three of us to watch tonight, we picked *Ronin* with Robert De Niro. Mattias and I lie on the couch and Rochelle has the armchair to herself. The three of us settle down to watch the film. Rochelle offered to go out and see some friends and leave us to it, but we were both happy for Rochelle to stay. It's nice they both get on well, it always helps when your friend and boyfriend get on. After the film, we say goodnight to Rochelle and head to bed.

I go into autopilot when I hear the alarm and get up and have a shower, with a horrible, sad feeling in my stomach.

We are sitting in the taxi to the airport and we both have heavy hearts looking out the window of the taxi, not speaking a word between us. Normally the taxi ride to the airport takes forever, but today it seems to go so quickly. Today of all days I wish it were the other way around, even if I stayed all day in the taxi not uttering a word it wouldn't bother me as I know he would be right here beside me. We get out of the taxi, and I help him with his stuff. I go to pay for the taxi, but as usual Mattias won't let me, and he pays for the taxi. We go into the airport, and I'm quite surprised it's not that busy, usually it's chaos. I queue with Mattias to check his stuff in. The line is small and moves quite quickly. Once that's done, we head to the restaurant and sit for a bit. I order tea and Mattias gets a coffee.

"I really wish you didn't have to go," I say sadly.

"I know. Me too, but I promise you, I will come back and see you. I love you, Chelle," he says, grabbing my hand across the table and looking into my eyes.

"I love you too," I say quietly, knowing that we might never see each other again, that this could be our final goodbye.

It's time for him to go to departures and this is where we must say our last goodbyes once and for all. I start to cry. My heart is breaking. He pulls me in close and cuddles me and kisses me tenderly on the head. He has sunglasses on, I wonder if that's so no one can see his eyes, I think to myself.

"I love you. I will call you every week. I promise," he says in a whisper, his voice sounding shaky.

"I love you, too," I say through blubbering tears.

We give each other one last squeeze and a lingering kiss and pull ourselves apart from one another knowing if we don't, Mattias will miss his flight.

"I love you," he says while stroking my face.

"I love you too."

I watch him walk away with tears flooding down my face. He turns around and gives me one last wave, with a sad smile and walks through boarding, I stand and watch until he's out of view. Just before he's gone, he turns back around once more and gives me a wave. I wave too and give a half smile. I walk to the ladies toilets in the airport to go and compose myself. I stand staring into the mirror, my eyes red, heavy and swollen from all the crying. A lady comes out of the cubicle to go wash her hands and gives me a sympathetic smile. I wonder to myself how many others have waved their other halves off and cried like this at the airport. I don't think I would have been the first or either the last.

I splash my face with some cold water and pat my face down with some tissues. *God, I look a mess*, I think to myself. I wish I had taken shades now, having to walk out the airport like this. *Och it's fine, nobody knows me*, I tell myself. I walk with my head down watching one foot then the other with a heavy heart, wondering if I will ever see him again.

I feel so sad inside, like my heart is broken. With every foot I put in front of the other, it feels like I'm doing it in slow motion.

Chapter Fifteen

May 2015 – 17 years later

Monday mornings are always the worst. Running around trying to get Niamh ready for school and myself ready for work.

"Come on chicken, you're going to be late, hurry up and finish your breakfast. We need to beat the morning traffic," I say while turning the television off.

"Och Ma. I was watching that," Niamh says.

"Well tough! Away you go and give your teeth a brush. It's just gone twenty past eight, so we need to get a move on."

I pick up her cereal bowl off the table and run it under the sink. As I turn around, she's standing there in front of me.

"Brushed them, Ma."

"You sure? That was awful quick," I say with a half-smile and roll of the eyes

"Look," she says with her mouth wide open.

"Okay. I believe you," I say while patting her on the head.

Before we leave for the day, I give Niamh a once over and fix her blazer and tie, then lock the door behind us. The journey to her primary school takes about five minutes in the car. She started school last August and enjoys going which is always a bonus. I park the car up and then walk her up to the school gates. It's the same as every day, we give each other a big cuddle and I tell her I love her and to have a good day.

"Bye Mummy."

"Bye chicken. Remember, Da will pick you up from school today."

She gives me a nod and then runs away to play with her friends, not looking back. I check my watch; it's now twenty to nine. I don't need to be at work till nine thirty which takes the pressure off. This gives me more time in the morning traffic to compose myself. Like most parents doing the school run I always feel harassed in the morning to get her there on time then to get myself to work.

Once Niamh came along, I spoke to my boss about starting later and he was very accommodating. To be frank I've got it good. Before I had Niamh, I used to live out of a suitcase most weeks, flying all over the world selling our famous "Dublin's finest" Irish whisky. I've worked for this company since I graduated from university, and in recent years it's grown double in size. I don't need to fly all over the place now, just when there is a big deal to close or if someone is off. I haven't been away for the last three years which has been good, as Niamh needs me at home. To be honest, I don't like being away from her for too long, I've become a bit of a home bird since she came along.

My phone starts ringing through the car's Bluetooth system – it's Shane.

"Hey, how's you? You were early leaving this morning. I don't think I heard you leave."

"Aye, I was early doors this morning. I had a lot of stuff to catch up on and wanted to go in early so that I could pick the wee one up from school on time. How was she going into school today?"

"She was grand. 'Bye, Mummy' and away she went to play with her friends."

"Oh good. Well, I better get back to it. Will see you at the house tonight after work."

"Aye, see you then. I made stew and potatoes so all you need to do is heat it up, but I should be home on time."

We both say our goodbyes and hang up. The traffic has been quite bad this morning, especially as it started raining, it seems like everyone is on the road. Coupled with the X1 I'm driving today is Shane's car, I don't normally drive his car. My wee Corsa does me fine but that's in the garage just now waiting on parts, so I must drive this big thing. I don't like driving it, I feel it's too big for me to park. Just as I'm pulling into the car park at work my boss' number appears on my screen.

"Morning Steve. I'm in the car park just parking up the car just now."

"Sure, you're fine. I just thought I would let you know. Cheryl MacLaughlan called you regarding the impending sale, she's wondering if you can give her a call on her mobile."

"Aye, no probs. Let me grab a pen and get the number off you as I don't think I have her direct mobile number." I grab my bag from the passenger seat and rummage through it to find many pens in my bag. I look through my bag once more to find a bit of paper to write the number down, but can't find a bit of paper. I then open the glove box stretching over to the passenger side to see if Shane has something in there I can write on

"Okay Steve, fire away with the number."

Once Steve's given me the number, I reach across to close the glove box, but another bit of paper gets stuck. I go to push it in and then something catches my eye. I read it: a receipt for the Central Hotel Donegal, not giving too much thought, I push it back in and close the glove box and grab my work stuff from the boot and head on into work. On my way into the office, I call my client Cheryl back to see what was so urgent. It was good news – she wants to up her order. Before I go to my desk, first things first, I need a coffee. I head to the coffee machine.

"Hey Jane, how are you?"

"Good thanks, Michelle. How's things with you?"

"Och alright for a Monday morning I suppose. Saturday and Sunday are the quickest days of the week."

"Oh, don't I know it." She grabs her coffee and heads off.

Once I get seated at my desk, I drink some coffee while waiting on my computer to load up. *Hmm that's good*, I think to myself, after the first sip of coffee goes down. I tend to get myself so stressed in the morning making sure myself and Niamh are up and organised and Niamh like all kids sometimes in the morning will just sit there and stare into space at the telly. It can be stressful, and I don't like getting on at her in the morning. I always feel that sets the two of us up for a bad day. To the left of my computer screen there is a photo of me, Niamh and Shane taken about two years ago when Niamh was three. I really like it as we are all smiling looking at the camera and there is a nice waterfall in the background of the photo. Just as I'm admiring the photo, Sinead, my assistant, pops her head in.

"Did you get the email, Michelle?"

"What email?"

"Steve has asked us all to attend a brief team meeting this morning."

"Sure, I'm just logging on now."

Sinead sits across the other side of the desk from me. She's very good at her job and very efficient. She's worked here for three years like me when she graduated, she came straight here. She's my younger self. She now travels the globe selling our brand. I do the groundwork finding potential clients, then I organise for her to go to whichever country the client is in and then do the last of the sales pitch. Usually by the time Sinead goes to them we kind of know it's ninety percent in the bag. It's a great job if you don't have kids and a family. I sometimes miss going to the airport and just flying away and then sitting at the bar on the way back and chatting and meeting random strangers. I also loved watching people and the world go by from afar.

I start to go through my inbox and reply to outstanding emails. Once I clear my feet with that, I move on to prepare a template for my next pitch to potential clients and then start my facts and figures. Before I realise the time, it's ten to eleven. I start making the long walk down the narrow corridor, with a load of the other staff to attend our team meeting, grabbing another coffee as I go.

"Right folks, thanks for attending. It's been a good bloody month: our sales are up, and we have a few potential new buyers," Steve says.

We go through the minutes of the last meeting and make sure we agree with everything and nothing is missed before we move on.

"As I said, we have a few potential new buyers with a big buyer in Sweden. Michelle, can you give us an update on that please?" Steve asks.

"Sure. So, I have started the groundwork with my client Mr Johansson. He is interested in a large order. Sinead is going over in three weeks to meet Eric and after that it should be a case of signing on the dotted line. We recently got two new clients, one in Scotland and one in New York. As Steve states, our sales are up and our figures are looking good, so well done everyone."

I sit back down as, even now I am older, I still don't like public speaking or being the focus of people's attention. I thought after all this time doing the job and being confident at what I do it would pass, but it never does.

Steve goes on to chat about next month's targets, sales and stats. He reminds us that at the end of the month, the company will put on a family day for all staff and their families at the Castlecomer, Discovery Park in Kilkenny. After this, we all start making our way back along the corridor to our desks.

"Michelle, I'm going out for lunch, do you want anything?" asks Sinead.

"No thanks. I brought something in. Thanks though," I say sincerely.

The day passes quite quickly and next thing I know, I'm packing up and heading home. I'm always in a rush to get home as the traffic is always bad at this time of night. I stay on the other side of Dublin on the outskirts in a place called Ranelagh, it's a quiet area and is great for kids with some great schools. Usually, this time of night when I'm driving home, I will give me folk a call or my friend Rochelle. She has her hands full now, as she has three young boys, who are all close in age. As all young boys are, they have ants in their pants and are into everything. When I meet poor Rochelle, she always looks exhausted. We organise play dates and, once in a blue moon, no kids, we go for lunch and some nice wine. I don't see her that often, as she stays on the other side of the city, but when I do it's like we just pick up where we left off.

My phone is ringing and it's Shane.

"Hey, everything okay at home?"

"Aye, everything is fine. What did you say about dinner tonight?"

Christ, I think to myself, *does he not listen to a word I say? I told him earlier what to do*. I then repeat that it was stew and just needs to be heated back up.

"Thanks Michelle, see you in a bit. Watch the roads," he says.

He must be a bit stressed. He's been working a lot lately and I think it's catching up on him. He has his own car dealership. It was a family business, his dad's, then he retired and passed it on to Shane. He was going to pass it on to both his sons but Gerry, his other son, had no interest in it and works in finance. Since his Da's retired, Shane's his own boss. It's not far from our house, which is great because if I get held up or anything he's a lot nearer to Niamh's school and because he's his own boss, he doesn't have to ask, he just lets his staff know. That's the beauty of being your own boss, you can do what you want, when you want. I've been seeing Shane now for ten years, we are engaged with no immediate plans to marry, we are quite happy the way we are. I met him when I went to buy a car and ended up walking out with a new car and his phone number, he was full of the patter and as folk say the rest is history.

"Hello, I'm home."

"Mummy!" Niamh jumps into my arms, as I pick her up and twirl her around.

"Hello chicken. How was your day today at school? What did you do today?"

She pulls me by the hand and takes me through to the kitchen. Pinned on the fridge is a picture of what looks like me, Niamh and Shane.

"Did you draw that?"

"Yes," she says with a big smile, nodding her head.

"Wow, that's so good. What a little star you are," I give her a tender kiss on her forehead.

"Hello," the voice coming from behind me is Shane. He leans in and gives me a kiss.

"Have you both eaten?" I ask.

"No, we were waiting for you. While we were waiting, I did Niamh's homework with her," Shane says.

I noticed Shane hadn't heated up dinner after calling me and asking what it was. I turn to the hob and start heating up the stew. Once it's all piping hot, I dish it onto our plates, and we all sit down to have dinner. During the week in our house, we have a nightly routine that doesn't change unless it's school holidays or the weekend, like most parents with young kids.

As tonight's dinner is stew, it can be a hit or a miss with Niamh: sometimes she likes it, sometimes she doesn't. It just depends what mood she's in. She ends up eating most of her dinner. Afterwards, I tidy up, clearing all the plates and stacking them in the dishwasher. While I'm cleaning up, Niamh goes through with her dad to watch some TV before bed. At seven, it's bath time for the little princess and I make sure the bath is full of bubbles and put her favourite bath toys in. Niamh then goes in the bath; I keep the door open so I can hear her playing while I sort her room for bedtime. I lay out her night clothes and close the curtains, pull the duvet back and put her little night lamp on at the side of her bed. She sleeps with that on all night. I must find Mr. Piggy, her treasured teddy, that she takes everywhere. Once that's all done, I get her out of the bath and ready and into her bed. I shout down to Shane to come up, as she likes us both to read to her at night-time, we read a few chapters and then we both give her a kiss goodnight, leaving the door a jar.

Shane and I both go downstairs and see what's on the TV. I've started watching soaps, does that mean I'm officially getting old, I think to myself. Long gone are my carefree days. Once I've had my fill of TV, I start the ironing; it's the one household task I hate doing but needs must and all that. Just after ten myself and Shane call it a night and head up to bed. I set my alarm clock for six thirty am, the same as any other school day. I go through and brush my teeth and when I come back through, Shane has already hung up his work stuff for the morning and is in bed already.

He rolls round to me and gives me a kiss good night then turns back around. I cuddle into him, while we chat about our day.

Before long, Shane is snoring next to me. I can't seem to get to sleep, I feel caught in my own thoughts, and Shane's snoring doesn't seem to help. I can't work out what's making me restless.

Chapter Sixteen

I'm woken by my alarm clock and as soon as I open my eyes, I can see the sun beaming into my bedroom window. It's going to be a nice day, I think to myself. I can already hear Shane downstairs pottering about in the kitchen. I get up and head downstairs to make myself a coffee. As I get down to the kitchen, Shane is making himself one.

"Morning. Do you want a coffee? The kettle has just boiled," he says while taking a sip from his cup.

"Yes, please, thanks," I lean over to kiss him; his lips meet mine and flashes me a smile.

I take my coffee from Shane and go sit at the kitchen table. I pull out my phone and have a quick read of my news app before I need to go for a shower.

Once I get out of the shower, I pop my head into Niamh's room.

"Morning chicken. Up you get," I say with a smile.

She gives a stretch and has a wriggle about the bed, but the look on her face tells me she's not impressed about having to move this morning.

"Come on, darling up you get," I say with a half sigh, hoping it's not going to be one of those days.

"Another five minutes mummy," Niamh pleads.

"Okay, five minutes."

I go in and get myself ready. Once I'm dressed, I go back through and get Niamh organised. Downstairs I quickly prepare her breakfast; it's like a military operation in the mornings. Niamh comes bounding down the stairs, straight to the living room to find the remote to put on her favourite cartoons. As soon as she finds it, I can hear Donald Duck blasting out the tv.

After dropping Niamh off at school, I'm just reversing into the car park at work when my phone rings.

"Hey Rochelle, how's it going?" I ask.

"So, Danny said I look exhausted and could do with a break, he said to give you a call and go chill out with you tomorrow and him and the boys will do something. Do you fancy it?" Rochelle asks excitedly.

"Aye, I will give Shane a call and see what he is up to tomorrow. As we haven't made any plans yet for Saturday. I was just going to take Niamh swimming. What do you fancy doing?"

"Go for some lunch and a couple of drinks, nothing heavy."

"Sure, that sounds grand. Will call Shane now and text you and let you know," I say warmly, thinking it's been a while since I've last had lunch with Rochelle.

"Grand Chelle. Speak to you soon."

I turn off my car ignition and fumble through my work bag to find my phone. Christ, I have everything in this bag except the kitchen sink – I really need to tidy it.

> Hey Rochelle called me and asked if I want to meet her tomorrow. Do you have any plans? Can you keep Niamh for a bit if you don't have anything planned? Xx

He will be rough tomorrow, that's a given. For several months now every Friday, he has been going to the local golf club, more to hold up the bar with his newfound friends than having a game of golf. I went a couple of times with him but found some of the people there snooty. Don't get me wrong, there is always a good atmosphere and some weekends a band will be playing. Although lately he has been going on Friday and Saturday. I know he works hard, and I do not mind as he needs time to unwind, but two nights is a bit excessive. Especially come Sunday, when he lies on the couch all day and nurses his weekend hangover. I feel it is partly my own fault it has got to this point. He used to ask me If I wanted to go with him, but most of the time my answer is no, so it got to the point where he just stopped asking me if I wanted to go to the golf club with him. I couldn't even use the excuse of a babysitter, as we have never had any problems. Our next-door neighbor's teenage daughter gets on well with Niamh and is always happy to make extra cash. *If Shane has something on tomorrow, I will ask Orla if she can watch Niamh for a few hours*, I think to myself.

I'm halfway through drafting a report when I hear my phone ting.

> Yea that's no worries me and Niamh can go into town and watch a film or something tomorrow. XX

Great. I quickly text a reply back to Rochelle.

We are on for tomorrow. 😊 xx

I manage to complete my report for lunchtime and am just sitting eating my lunch when young Sinead comes back in with hers and sits down at her desk.

"What's your plans this weekend, Michelle?" Sinead asks.

"I'm meeting my pal tomorrow, gonna go for some lunch and a couple of drinks. What about yourself, any plans?"

"I'm having a quiet one tonight and then hitting the town tomorrow with a few friends. I'm going to look for holidays tonight for me and the girls. We fancy Ibiza or Greece," she says.

"Girls' holiday – that could be messy!" I exclaim.

"I know," Sinead says letting out a laugh and giving a raise of her eyebrows.

"I went to Ibiza years ago with ma pals and I had the best time. They took me there to cheer me up."

"Why, what was wrong?" Sinead asks and fully turns her body to me.

I've got Sinead's undivided attention now and she puts down her half-eaten sandwich and looks straight at me.

"Come on, spill?"

"Years ago, way before I met Shane. I was dating a guy and fell head over heels for him," I say, reminiscing.

"What happened?" Sinead jumps in to ask me the question before I can finish what I'm saying.

"He lived abroad, he worked here all summer and then at the end of the season, he went back home. We kept in touch when he went back home, we would take turns calling each other once a week," I then laugh while remembering something funny my dad used to do.

"What are you laughing at?" Sinead asks, intrigued.

"Me Da used to answer the phone to him and shout 'Chelle,

Sweden calling'." I wave my hand around in the shape of a telephone back and forth, showing Sinead the hand gesture me Da used to do when Mattias was on the other end of the phone.

"I always laugh when I think of my Da shouting Sweden calling. He used to remind me of Terry Wogan at the Eurovision song contest," I smile while remembering back. As I turn back to face Sinead again, I notice she has a bewildered look on her face, like what I have said has just gone way over her head.

"Terry Wogan is an Irish treasure; he did the Eurovision for years and his famous lines was 'nil point'. I loved being young with my sister sitting down to watch the Eurovision, always in the month of May. With my aunty and mother, and all of us would get a Chinese takeaway to sit and munch on while watching it. My Da would often shout get that shit off the TV. To which my Ma and aunty would tell him to bugger off. The outfits were all so over the top and the older I got, the more I guessed it was politically motivated, and I started to get a good idea what way some of the countries would vote, but good old Terry Wogan saved the day. Think we all watched it for Terry's charm. When a country would call in, Terry would always say Finland calling or so on and so on," I explain to Sinead. She still looks a bit dumbfounded.

"Only women of a certain age will know Terry Wogan and the golden era of the Eurovision, Sinead. You are a bit too young," I say laughing but not having the energy to explain any more to Sinead; the moment's gone. She was born in the wrong decade to fully understand and see the funny side.

"Getting back to the Swede. That's a shame, did you both just drift apart or what?" Sinead asks.

"He got offered a decent job in Sweden and knew he wouldn't be able to come back in the summertime. I couldn't go over there because I still had my studies. We promised to keep in touch, but you know how it is. Just dwindled off, we remained friends for a bit and wrote to each other, then one day we both just stopped writing and calling each other, it just fizzled out and we just never heard from one another again," I say pulling a sad face.

"That's a shame, have you ever got back in touch with him or looked him up on Facebook?"

"Nah, I believe what's in the past shouldn't be dragged up again. No point looking back and opening old doors that are supposed to remain closed," I say firmly.

"Come on, let's have a nosy." Sinead starts pulling out her phone. "What's his name?"

"Och don't be daft, Sinead, I don't want to look him up," I say.

"Come on, are you not even one bit curious? You know what they say, curiosity killed the cat," she says, nudging my arm.

What does he look like now? Is he happy? Is he married? Does he have kids? Lots of questions flash before me and I find myself wanting to know the answers.

"Okay. His name is Mattias Ludvig Karlsson," I say laughing, unable to believe I am being talked into this.

"Jesus. That's a bloody mouthful," Sinead says.

"Ludvig was his middle name, but I don't know if he will use that on his social media account."

Sinead types everything in and stares at her screen for a few moments, waiting for the results.

"Right, we have loads of Mattias Karlssons," she says, not lifting her head up from her phone.

"Let's see, let's see," I say feeling a bit impatient now.

Sinead hands me over the phone and I start scrolling down all the profile pictures on screen. I get halfway down.

"There he is," I say with a smile. I can't hide my face lightening up.

I click on the profile and start spying on his account. He looks good, slightly older than when I last saw him, which is to be expected. A few wrinkles around the eyes, I can relate to that I think to myself, it happens to the best of us. He still has that beautiful full mop of hair that most women would like to run their hands through. He's smiling at the camera, with that beautiful white smile that takes up half his face, just how I remember. Either side of him are two young boys– one of them looks just like him. I click on his pictures and have a scroll through them, there are a few with friends and holiday pictures. I click on his personal profile but that all seems private except that he still lives in Sweden. Going through his social media account, I get the impression he doesn't really use Facebook so often. I have one more look at his profile picture. Those two young boys must be his children, I say to Sinead.

"He looks happy, I'm pleased for him. I could imagine he would be a good dad. That's nice, you've put my curiosity to bed," I say while handing Sinead back her phone, for her to cast her eye over him also.

Sinead is now checking out his Facebook account. "He's hot, Michelle, I can see why you liked him. I wonder if he has ever looked at your social media?"

"You've got me on Facebook, he would never find my account. I have all my settings private, with all the scammers and weirdos you come across on the internet. Plus, I don't live in Cobh anymore. I have my location in Dublin and my username is Chelledoo," I explain knowing how ridiculous 'Chelledoo' sounds.

I pack up for the day and head out to my car and start the long drive home in this heat. Although I shouldn't complain, it's not often we get nice weather. I turn on radio two and 'Viva Forever' is on the radio, I sing away to the lyrics and it makes me smile. Thinking of the good times I had with the girls, when we were all young and Spice Girl mad. After today, looking at Mattias' social media account, my thoughts drift to him also, when we were in my dad's car many years ago, singing along to this song. After snooping at his Facebook account, it feels a bit like a deja vu moment that the same song would come on. That's the great thing about music, it can transport you back in time to a place, feeling or person. I think once more about Mattias and how happy he looked in the photo. I genuinely feel happy for him.

I don't like the next song that comes on, so I change the settings on my dashboard and put on my playlist that I was listening to this morning. I am stopped in traffic and feeling a bit sticky in this heat. I hate waiting in traffic. I need a cheap dopamine boost, to distract my mind from queuing in traffic. I quickly squint through my playlist for a second, careful not to take my eyes off the road for too long and pick a dance track, 'Make the World Go Round' by Sandy B. If this doesn't pick me up nothing will.

Chapter Seventeen

Rushing through Dublin's cobble streets, I nearly trip up as I go, what with the high heels I have on. I'm fifteen minutes late meeting Rochelle at a new cocktail bar Peruke & Periwig on Dawson Street in the centre of town. To make matters worse, the heavens have just opened, and I never took a brolly with me. *Only in bloody Ireland*, I think to myself, *can it be so nice yesterday when I'm at work and then pissing down today*. Before I left the house this morning, I had straightened my hair perfectly. The new straightening irons are the best invention to happen in the early noughties. They actually straighten my hair, and I don't have to wait thirty minutes until they heat up. However, when I finally get to Rochelle, my lovely straight hair will be matted curls in this rain.

"Hey how are ya?" Rochelle says getting up out of her chair to give me a cuddle.

"I'm good, thanks. Except for looking like a drowned rat, I was rushing out the door and forgot to take my brolly," I say holding up my wet hair.

I throw my jacket over the spare chair beside us.

"I'm just going to the toilet to dry my hair off with the hand dryer."

"No worries, I will look at the menu and see what cocktails they have," Rochelle says.

"Okay, but I'm going to eat something and have a cocktail, I don't want to drink on an empty stomach, or I will be gaga."

Once I've half dried my hair, I check myself in the mirror and give myself a once over before going back into the bar to join Rochelle, who hands me the menu.

"What's the menu like?" I ask.

"It looks good, I think I'm going to go for the prawn linguini and a porn star martini," Rochelle says, passing me the menu.

Just then the waitress comes over, I ask her to give us a few extra minutes 'till I look at the menu. I study it but feel it's too early in the day to get a starter and a main so just go for the same as Rochelle, sometime later the waitress comes back and takes our order.

"So how are you Chelle? I feel like we've not chatted for ages."

"I'm good, just been extremely busy at work and juggling Niamh's after school stuff. I feel like there's not enough hours in the day. What about you?"

"Oh, just running mad after the four of them. Sometimes I feel like I've got four young boys, with Danny. Josh is being potty trained just now and I'm carrying a potty with me everywhere I go," she says laughing.

"Does he not give you much of a hand with the boys? Is everything okay with you and Danny?" I ask, concerned.

"No, I'm joking, everything is grand. It's just I've got the three of them shouting 'Ma, Ma, Ma' every two seconds. Then Danny will be like 'where's ma jeans, can you iron my shirt.' I just get pissed off every so often and need a moan."

In between chatting the waitress brings over our pornstar martinis.

"They look nice. Sláinte to us," Rochelle says lifting her glass to meet mine.

"Sláinte. This is long overdue," I say smiling, glad that I am finally catching up with my old pal.

"So how are Niamh and Shane?"

"Niamh is grand, she's a right wee trooper, she's getting on well at school. Shane's fine, busy with work." I say rolling my eyes.

"That doesn't sound good. What's going on Chelle, is everything okay?"

"Och, yes, he's always on the go at work. Then at the weekends he's taken up a new hobby, golf. Although I think he spends more time in the club house at the bar than playing golf," I say flatly.

"Put your bloody foot down there, Chelle," Rochelle says with her face getting redder and redder as though you can almost see the anger rising from within.

"I don't want to be one of those partners where you say you can't do this, and you can't do that and sound needy. I just feel that two nights at the weekend is just a bit excessive, I don't feel I'm being unreasonable, do you?" I ask.

"Absolutely feckin not. If Danny did that to me, hell would freeze," she says giving a laugh that's funnier than the sentence.

Just then our lunch comes over and it looks and smells delicious. The waitress asks if we want any black pepper or any other drinks.

"Yeah, can we have two house white wines please?" I ask.

"Chelle, we've not even finished our cocktails yet," Rochelle says disapprovingly.

"I know, but I like a glass of white wine with seafood."

Rochelle gives a roll of the eyes and says whatever.

Although she doesn't say it, I can tell what she's thinking. Oh, a glass of white wine with seafood, who do I think I am?

As the afternoon passes, we both appear a bit merry with the alcohol we've consumed, and I feel happy and content, for catching up with my oldest friend, talking away my worries. She also appears happy and relaxed talking about hers.

"We should do this more often Rochelle."

"Aye, we definitely should," she says with a warm smile.

"Oh, I knew I had something to tell you," I say giggling like a teenager.

I tell Rochelle about work yesterday and how Sinead convinced me to look up Mattias on social media and he appeared to have two children now and looked happy in the photo. Rochelle reminds me, you can never really tell what's true and what's not from social media. Everyone wants to put it out there that they have a great life and are living the dream, but the reality away from social media is very different behind closed doors. No life or relationship is picture perfect, everyone has their ups and downs. She laughs and asks if he is still hot.

Rochelle gets up to go to the toilet and I can't tell if it's because of the dim light in the bar or the tables being so close together that she's tripped up, or if it's the alcohol she's consumed. She darts her head around the room to see if anyone saw her trip and gives me a look and a laugh and heads to the toilet. The barman stares at Rochelle to see what she's up to. Rochelle picked a window seat, if she's anything like me it will be for the people watching. The red curtains that hang either side of the windows are pulled back onto a brass stopper so you can see outside to the street. It's now gone teatime, and the street outside is still packed with people. I look round the cock tail bar now that am alone to study the place. All the paintings on the wall each catch my eye, particularly the one with a lady's portrait. I'm staring at it before I realise Rochelle has come back from the toilet and is just pulling the chair out to sit back down.

"Chelle. I'm a bit merry, I think I will get a taxi home."

"Yeah me too. I'm quite tired," I say in between yawning.

We grab our jackets and bags and walk up to the bar to pay our bill. We split the bill and leave a tip and exit out the main doors onto the street.

"Where are you going Rochelle, the taxi rank is that way," I say with a laugh and shake my head.

"Oh, the fresh feckin air has hit me. I feel like I've had one too many," she says, giggling.

We walk through Dublin's streets to the nearest taxi rank. We give each other a hug and say our goodbyes. Rochelle goes in the first taxi, and I go in the second.

I arrive back at the house, and I can see Naimah and Shane sitting watching the TV through the window as I walk up our path.

"Hello," I shout as I open the door.

"Mummy!" Niamh shouts from the couch.

"Alright, how are you? I wasn't expecting you in till later," Shane says.

"I'm grand," I say with a slur in my words.

Shane gives out a laugh. "I think your mother's merry, Niamh."

Niamh stares blankly wondering what merry means.

"I'm bursting for the toilet," I exclaim, while nearly pushing Shane off his feet to get past him and up the stairs. *Oh, what a relief*, I think to myself. My old nan used to have a saying when she needed the toilet, she was away to spend a penny. Every woman who has given birth knows that when you have a few drinks, the minute you break the seal, you're up and down to the toilet all night long.

"So, what did you two get up to today?" I ask Niamh.

"We went to the swing park and Daddy pushed me really high on the swings."

"That sounds like you had great fun."

"Yeah, and someone didn't want to leave the swings when it was time to go. They went in a wee huff," Shane says and turns his head to Niamh with a smile. Niamh pulls a shy face.

"What did the two of you have for dinner?" I ask.

Before Shane can talk Niamh butts in excitedly. "We had a McDonald' and I got a happy meal with this wee toy," Niamh pulls out a figure from the latest Disney film to be released.

"Grand, it sounds like you both had a nice day. Shall we go swimming tomorrow, the three of us?"

"Yeah, why not," Shane says and looks to Niamh for her reaction, but she's back engrossed playing with her new toy.

I get up off the couch to go through to the kitchen to make myself a coffee. I'm about to shout through to Shane to see if he wants a coffee, but before I can he's walking into the kitchen. He comes up behind me and puts his arms around me and gives me a kiss on the cheek and we linger there for a minute. I sense he's wanting to ask me something but is picking his time.

"How was Rochelle?"

"Yea, she's good. She's kept busy with the kids. I'm making a coffee, you want one?"

"Nah. You're fine. Connor texted earlier to see if I wanted to go for a few pints tonight. I said I would see what time you came back at and if it wasn't too late then maybe..."

There it is. That's what he really came through to ask.

"You're out most weekends with your newfound friends at the club house, can you not just stay in with me and Niamh tonight?"

He looks at me with the pleading puppy eyes and I can tell he's wanting to go with his friends.

"Do what you want," I say coldly.

Shane walks away with his head down and pulls out his phone obviously to start texting Connor to say he will be there. Maybe I should feel bad for saying that, but I don't feel bad. If it were just once in a blue moon, then no issue but not every weekend. I make myself a coffee and go back through to the living room, where Niamh is now sitting with her tablet playing a game and Shane is staring blankly at the tv.

"I texted Connor and said I would see him next week," he says while looking impassively at his phone which appears to be vibrating now.

"Oh right," I say, not giving much of a response.

When a woman says "do what you want" to a man, the man usually knows that the woman is pissed off and if they do in fact do what they want, then hell will probably freeze over, and he will be in the doghouse for the next number of days. *Well, that worked*, I think to myself.

I take Niamh's tablet off her and ask her if she wants to watch a film. Niamh picks Frozen.

No sooner has the film started, Shane is texting back and forth on his phone. He's looking a bit stressed.

"Are you alright? Is Connor annoyed with ya? You see him most weekends, surely he can't be angry?"

"Am grand. Aye Connor is like my second wife. He forgets I have you and Niamh," he says laughing.

"Just turn your phone off."

"I've told him to stop being a baby, he can go one night without seeing me."

We both laugh.

Chapter Eighteen

I wake up the next morning groggy from the previous day's antics with Rochelle and still feel a bit sleepy in the morning. I'm convinced it's because the blinds I have in my bedroom are black out blinds so come summer or winter if they are down, you really do need a bomb to go off before you wake. You're not woken up by the light early mornings. I usually only put my blinds down at the weekends, as I'm terrified I will sleep in during the week.

Shane turns round and gives me a cuddle and kiss.

"Morning," Shane says then pulls me in close to him.

"Morning," I say, still half asleep.

Just then the door burst opens and in Niamh comes, jumping up on to the bed.

"Good morning, chicken, did you have a good sleep?" I say while giving her a cuddle.

"Yes, Ma. Da, when are we all going swimming today?"

"Jesus, Niamh, we haven't even had breakfast yet. I wish I had your energy," he says and grabs Niamh and tickles her.

While we are all lying in bed, Niamh tells us about a dream

she had last night and how she was a princess, and a dragon was chasing her. I laugh to myself and think kids are great: they have the best imaginations. Folk should look at the world through a five-year-old's eyes at least once.

"I'm hungry," Niamh says, looking at us both with her big blue eyes.

Shane and I both look at each other to see who is going to say first, 'Come on and I will get you some breakfast'. We don't say anything but we both know what the other is thinking.

"Come on then, I'll get you some breakfast," I say with a half-hearted sigh.

"I'll be down in a minute," Shane says while stretching out in bed.

"It's fine. I will see to her, what do you want for breakfast?" I ask Shane.

"Whatever's going, I'm not fussy."

I go downstairs and as I walk through to the kitchen, the light is beaming already and shines right on to the cupboard which only highlights that I need to bleach them. *Oh god, I better do that later*, I think to myself, *that doesn't look very good.* I open my kitchen window and look out; there is not a cloud in the sky and the sun is already high. It's a beautiful day for the start of June. It's hard to believe it was such a terrible day yesterday. Always the same whenever I try and make any plans.

"It's going to be a cracker today, Niamh."

"What is, Ma?"

"The weather. It looks like it's going to be a lovely day." Niamh turns and looks out the window.

I head over to the fridge and have a look in it to see what there is.

"Do you want cereal, or French toast?"

"Can I have French toast, please?"

"Of course. Come on through and I will put the telly on for you while you're waiting."

I go through to the living room and open both blinds and put the telly on for Niamh and flick through a couple of the kid's channels. She settles with Tom and Jerry. I go back through and heat up the oven and take out sausages and bacon for Shane to have and then start beating eggs for the French toast. While I'm cooking breakfast, I can hear Shane walking around upstairs. A few moments later, he gives me a kiss on the neck and puts his arms around me.

"Something smells nice, what are you cooking?"

"I've got a fry up on for you and some French toast on for her ladyship."

"Are you not having anything?"

"Yeah. Although, I'm trying to be good so I'm going to have cereal," I say pulling a face. A fry up does sound much more appealing, but the other day when I was getting ready for work my work trousers felt a bit tight and when I looked in the mirror, I thought my tummy was getting bigger. In my head I then heard one of Kate Moss' most famous sayings "nothing tastes as good as skinny feels." So I thought there and then, I better start cutting out the junk and all the biscuits at work.

"Sure, there's nothing to you, it's Sunday. The lord's day of rest. Get yourself something else," Shane says while trying to lift me up.

"No, I told you I'm being good," I give him a smile.

Later in the day after we've taken Niamh swimming, Shane decides to have a BBQ with the weather being so good and calls his family and asks them if they want to come round and join us. His Ma, Da and his Ma's mum all decide to come round. He asked his brother and his family, but they said it was short notice as they'd already taken stuff out for tea. I then frantically start cleaning the house before they all came over. Niamh goes to the shop with her Da to get the BBQ stuff.

A while later, Niamh bursts in the door. "Mammy, Mammy look what Daddy bought me, he got me a paddling pool."

"Oh wow, aren't you lucky. We will need to get it set up."

"Michelle, can you give us a hand with some of the shopping?"

I follow Shane out to the car and when I see the boot open, I have a look inside the car, and realise he's bought shopping for the five thousand.

"Jesus Shane, who's all coming to this barbie?"

Shane laughs as he struggles with carrying a load of bags. I grab some and follow him in.

"Right, I will go and set up Niamh's paddling pool then get the BBQ sorted," Shane says while opening the fridge to take out a beer.

"Okay, I'm just finishing off cleaning the house then I will be out to join you both."

While I'm cleaning the bathroom, the window is open, I can hear Niamh laughing from down in the back garden. I hurry up and finish to get down and join them.

As I go to the patio door into our back garden, Shane has set the pool up for Niamh and she's splashing around having the time of her life. Shane is up at the far corner on our patio starting to light up the barbie.

"I will go and fire the chicken and stuff in the oven. What time are they coming over at?" I ask.

"Sure, they said three o'clock."

I then check my watch and it's twenty past two. "Right, I will go and get started in the kitchen."

I heat the oven to half cook the chicken and other bits to put in the oven first and then to finish off on the BBQ. Last thing I want is to give everyone food poisoning. While I'm waiting on the oven heating up, I go and start chopping the lettuce, cucumber, and tomatoes, and once they are all chopped, I put them in a bowl and cover it and put back in the fridge.

I can hear the front door opening and what sounds like Shane's mum shouting hello.

"Hi Bella, I'm through here," I shout back while putting the chicken in the oven.

Shane's Ma, Da and granny make their way through.

"Hello," I say to them all and go round each of them giving them a hug.

"Where's the rest of them?" Shane's Da, Kenny asks.

"Oh, they're both out in the garden, Shane said Gerry isn't coming," I say while pointing to the back garden where all you can hear is Niamh giggling.

"What can I get you all to drink?"

"Me and Jean will take tea please, Michelle," Shane's mum says.

"Bella's driving so I'll have a beer," Shane's Da says.

"Grand. You all head out and I will take it out to you all," I say while I finish off washing the dishes.

I prepare everyone's drinks then transfer them all on to a tray and head out. As I get outside, Niamh is still playing in the paddling pool. Shane, his parents and gran are all sitting around the table at the back of the garden near to the BBQ. When I walk past Niamh with the drinks, she starts splashing me.

"Oi, cheeky. I don't want to get wet," I say with a half serious face.

As the day goes on, everyone is appearing to enjoy themselves. Niamh is out of the paddling pool and dried off. We are all sitting around the patio table and enjoying our food. All that can be heard is the chewing of food, even Niamh is quietly sitting chewing on her burger. The sun has moved over the house and is beating down on the back garden. I have turned my chair slightly outward facing away from the table to catch the heat of the sun, hoping for a tan. Niamh comes and as she sits on my knee all I can smell is the sun lotion I put on her earlier mixed with the smell of BBQ food.

"Mummy after school tomorrow, can I play in the paddling pool again?"

"Of course. If the weather is like this then absolutely."

"Do you like school Niamh? Is everyone nice to you?" Shane's gran Jean asks Niamh. Shane's gran has always been a cute old lady. She's one of those old ladies that you just want to pick up, cuddle and take home with you.

"I like school, I have a friend called Annie and I like Miss Brennan," Niamh says matter of fact.

Shane and his dad are sitting at the other side of the table talking cars and business. All I can hear is sales, models, and figures.

Chapter Nineteen

I'm walking past reception heading up to my office, with the Monday morning blues, like most of Ireland on a Monday morning. As much as I love my job, I get the work blues every so often, more so when the weather is lovely the last place you want to be is sweating in an office. I think it's because we don't often get nice weather and when we do, we as a nation make the most of it, or at least that is what I tell myself.

"Michelle, Michelle!" I hear my name being called out and turn around to see Courtney, our receptionist, shouting me. I walk back to speak to her.

"Yeah, Courtney what's up?" I ask.

"It's Sinead, she called in this morning. She said she won't be in; she's broken her leg at the weekend and she's in plaster!" Courtney says with concern in her voice.

"Oh god, I hope she's alright. Did she say how she done it? I hope she wasn't dancing on the tables and went over her ankle!" I say with a laugh.

"No, she never. She said she would call yourself and Steve later," Courtney says with a raise of her eyebrows.

"Ah, okay thanks Courtney," I walk back up the stairs.

I see Steve in his office and wonder if he knows about Sinead. I head on down the corridor to his office door and give it a knock as his door is closed.

"Come in. Hi Michelle, what can I do for you?" Steve asks in his usual friendly tone.

"Hey. I've just come in and Courtney shouted me over to tell me about Sinead, did she tell you?"

"Aye she sure did. Poor soul is going to be off her feet for at least eight weeks. I said she can pop into the office from time to time if she feels like she's going mad. I'm glad you mentioned it as that was what I was wanting to speak to you about," he says with a coy smile.

"Aye what's up?" I ask anxiously, having a good idea what Steve is going to ask me next.

"I know you don't like overnights now, since Niamh came along, but now that Sinead has broken her leg, I really need you to tie up that deal in Sweden next week," he says, pulling his hands up to make the prayer sign.

"Aye, sure, how long will I be away for? Just so I can sort childcare and say to Shane?" I let out a slight sigh.

"Four nights. You'd leave on the Thursday and back the Monday," he says smiling, now knowing that I'm going to go.

"Why so long?" I ask.

"I need you to do a bit of wining and dining with them and work your Michelle magic. Also, the flights aren't great from Ireland to Sweden so unless you want an around the world trip to get back. There's direct returns on those days. You can relax for a day or two, get some sightseeing and shopping in," he says trying to win me over in his best sales pitch voice.

"Grand. Will go call Shane and me Ma. I would rather be home with Niamh and Shane than sightseeing," I say flatly to Steve.

I'm about to leave Steve's office but just remember one thing and about turn again.

"Did she say how she done it?"

Steve laughs. "Well, I think there was a lot of booze consumed and she was wearing high heels and went right over her ankle. However she couldn't get back up and the ambulance had to be called. Sinead said she wasn't drunk but I'm not entirely sure I believe her."

"Oh, right I will maybe give her a phone or a text later."

I leave the office this time and make my way to my own room. I walk to my window and open the blinds and log onto my computer. I use the office phone to call Shane and let him know what's happened and what I shall be expected to do. His phone just rings out, so I leave a voice mail asking him to give me a call. I think I better call my Ma also as she's not heard from me in a few weeks now, and I know she will come up and stay while I'm away to give Shane a hand with Niamh.

I dial me Ma's number and it takes a few rings before me Da answers.

"Hi Da, how are you?"

"I'm grand Chelle. How are the three of you?"

"We're all good Da. We had a BBQ yesterday with the weather being nice. Much doing with you all?"

"Not a thing. Your brother has a new girlfriend now. I can't keep up with him and his love life. There's a new one every couple of months," he says laughing.

"Oh well he's kept busy then," I say.

"That he is. We had Shannon's two staying over the weekend while her and Liam went to Scotland for the weekend, they were going to see some show in Edinburgh. I can't remember the name of it."

"Oh, that would have been nice for you both. Is Ma about Da, I'm on the scrounge and need to ask her something. I'm just calling quickly from work," I say feeling bad at cutting my Da short, but if I didn't, I would be on the phone to him for ages.

"Aye sure will just get her. Speak to you soon love," my Da says in his gentle tone.

"Hi love. How are you, what's wrong?" Me Ma asks.

Whenever I call my mum and say to my dad, I need to ask her something, my mother always automatically thinks there is something wrong.

"Nothing Ma. I've got a favour to ask you," I quickly tell her about Sinead and how that I know a week on Thursday would be short notice, but if there was any way she could help me and Shane with childcare for Niamh.

"Sweden, what part of Sweden are you going to?" she asks, probing.

"Stockholm, Ma."

There's a pause on the line.

"Ma, you still there?"

"Yes, sorry. Oh lovely, sure I will watch the wee one," she says quietly.

"Thanks Ma. Will you come stay with us the Wednesday, as I need to get to the airport early on the Thursday?"

"Aye, that's fine," she says warmly.

We quickly catch up on what's been happening with both of us. I ask after my brother and sister and any more news they have for me from home.

"Right Ma, I'm at work I better get back to it. Will give you a call at the weekend."

I start replying to emails and write to my client in Sweden to inform them the change of plan and that it will in fact be myself coming now. I email Steve to find out the itinerary for Sweden, no sooner have I emailed him, he sends me back all the details and asks me to contact the relevant companies to change

Sinead's name to my name. I scan through the itinerary and look at the accommodation that I will be staying in. When I used to be a regular flier and flew all over the place that was the first thing I would check – if it was a nice hotel or a shitty one. I would then use google to see what was around about the area in case I had any free time, to see a bit of the place and not just the hotel room and lobby. *This doesn't look bad*, I think to myself. They had Sinead booked into The Sheraton in Stockholm. I check what's nearby and read some reviews. A DJ plays for a couple of hours on a Friday and Saturday in the bar, central location, and a ten-minute walk to the old town.

"Perfect," I say to myself.

I contact The Sheraton and let them know it's a change of person and explain the reasons why, before contacting the airline and again changing the ticket.

My phone rings while I am in the middle of sorting out my name change with the airlines. I pop it on silent and see it is Shane. Once I finally get through to Ryan Air, I explain it's a name change and then pay the difference with the company credit card.

"Hi Shane, sorry we keep missing each other. I was calling you earlier to tell you, I've got to go to Sweden next Thursday as Sinead has fallen and broken her leg. I've asked my Ma to come through to give you a hand with Niamh the days you are working."

There's a silence on the line for a bit before Shane speaks. "Ah oh right, I see. You don't need to ask yer Ma to stay. I'm sure me and Niamh will be fine."

"Well, I just thought for the weekdays, you will need to get to work early and plus my Ma's not seen Niamh in a couple of weeks."

"I suppose, I never thought of the weekday early mornings."

"Do you not want my Ma to stay?" I ask feeling a bit upset.

"No, don't be daft. I like yer Ma, I just thought me and Niamh would be fine, but you're right, I'm forgetting about the weekdays."

We say our goodbyes and hang up.

I check my watch and see it's just gone twenty past ten and think to myself it's coffee time. I head out of my office into the staff room. I sit at one of the tables and type out a text to Sinead.

Hope you're okay and not in too much pain.
If you need anything call me xx

A short time later I receive a reply from Sinead.

Thanks Michelle. I'm okay, going to be a
long eight weeks. I heard you've got to go to
Sweden in my place now, sorry xx

Don't worry these things can't be helped. It's
been ages since I've been away so will be
nice getting out of the office. Talk soon and
take care xx

As I lift my coffee cup up to take a sip of it, the strong aroma smells delicious and as I take my first sip the warmth stings my lips. I feel the first few hot drops hit my tummy.

Mark our accountant walks in, he has the same idea as me and heads straight for the coffee.

"Can't beat a coffee in the morning, Mark, can ya?"

"You sure can't, Michelle," he says with his head down looking at his phone, not even lifting it to give me eye contact, which I find a bit rude.

He then pours his coffee and heads over to the other staff table, still with his head down on his phone.

I sit sipping my coffee thinking this is awkward, thinking back to my younger days at McLafferty's when all the staff would come into the staff room and wouldn't speak or would talk to each other in their own tongue. I've never felt like that here before, I don't know why I'm feeling like that now. Maybe I'm just being a little over sensitive.

"Did you have a good weekend, Mark? Did you get up too much?"

Mark finally puts down his phone and looks at me to give me his full attention.

"Grand, Michelle. I had a few rounds of golf with the boys on the Sunday and then we stayed back and had a few beers later at the clubhouse. Nothing heavy I knew I was coming in here today. What about yourself?"

"Yeah, I had a nice weekend. Met my pal on the Saturday and with the weather being so nice on the Sunday, we got the barbecue out. I didn't realise you were into golf; Shane, my partner, plays too," I say.

"I know Shane, I've seen him a couple of times at the club house."

"Oh, right he's never said," I say, puzzled that Shane's never mention it.

"Aye, yeah I've not saw him for the last wee while. Anyway, Michelle I better be making a move back to the grind," he says while picking up his coffee and tucking in his chair.

"See ya, Mark."

Shane's never told me he knows Mark, I think to myself. *That's odd, I thought he would say.*

I finish the rest of my coffee and head back along to my office. No sooner have I sat at my seat, Steve comes in.

"Michelle, can we please go through potential clients and look at the trends for last month?"

"Sure, Steve not a problem. Let me grab a note pad and I will be right through," I say while finishing off an email.

Steve grabs his printouts from the printer and hands a copy to me and we start going through the stats.

"I closed a deal with a client last week in the south coast of England. They were being a bit tricky; I said I would support them, and that they didn't need to buy a big order, to see how things go and then we would look at it again in six weeks," I say almost robotic as my mind appears to be elsewhere.

"That's great Michelle. I have been talking to a couple of potential clients in New York and like you I've also said we can support them by marketing the drink to their customers and scaling back on first order to see how it sells. Did you sort everything for Sweden?"

"Yes, everything is in place with name change and childcare," I say with a smile that really represents the fact I'm always one step ahead, and don't need to be asked twice.

We chat back and forth about other projects in the pipeline, and we look over more stats. When we have been through everything, I get up and leave to go back to my own office. As I sit back down at my desk the glare of the sun is so bright, I get up and pull the blinds down so that I can see my computer screen. I bury my head down in work that I've got to do and try and get a head as I know I'm not going to be in the office for most of next week now.

Chapter Twenty

On my drive back home thankfully, the traffic isn't too busy. *Everyone must be out enjoying the good weather*, I think to myself, the usual commute rush hour doesn't feel so bad. It helps the sun is beaming in the sky and the tunes I have blaring out my radio. As I'm slowing down in traffic, I put the window down and a nice cold breeze comes in through the car. This helps as I feel a bit sweaty from being in my work clothes all day and commuting back and forth. Cher comes on through the radio, 'Believe,' nothing like good old Cher to get you through the drive home.

When I arrive back at the house, I shout, "Hello." Normally there is a familiar voice shouting back, but I don't hear anyone, so I walk right through the house to the kitchen. I can see Shane and Niamh playing in the garden.

"Hello, you two," I shout from the back door and walk up to them at the other end of the garden. The two of them are playing with a water pistol and Niamh is screaming with laughter.

"Hey," Shane shouts while running after Niamh who has just soaked him.

"Mummy!" Niamh runs right up and soaks me.

"No, don't. Please don't, I'm in my work clothes," I say while putting my hands across my face and turning the other way.

"Right Niamh. I am gonna speak to your Ma. I will come back out and play with you in a bit," Shane says laughing.

Niamh isn't listening to what her Da is saying, she's too busy trying to soak the neighbor's cat with the water pistol.

"Don't scare the neighbour's cat, Niamh," I shout.

Shane and I go inside.

"How was work today?" Shane asks.

"Grand. I was just sorting out stuff for when I go away next week and keeping on top of everything especially now that Sinead is off."

"Sweden will be nice. I'm sorry if you thought I didn't want your Ma over. I didn't mean the way it came out," Shane says while giving me a hug.

I embrace Shane for a while and snuggle into his arms. "All I will probably see when I go away is four walls in a hotel room and offices during the day. The weather is great here, I would rather be home with you two," I say sadly.

"I know," Shane leans closer and gives me a kiss on the forehead.

"Oh, I forgot to say. The accountant Mark, he said he knows you through the golf club?"

Shane turns towards the cupboards looking for something "Oh right. I can't think who that would be. Where's the coffee?"

"It's there, staring right at you," I say while pulling out the coffee and holding it up to Shane's face, laughing.

"Christ, I think I'm needing glasses," he says.

Later that night I whip up a salad for the three of us and we sit out in the garden having our dinner, catching the last sun rays of the evening. Niamh decides to pick out all the tomatoes from her salad and leaves them to the side.

"Right chicken, it's time for bath and bed."

I'm literally gob smacked as without any fuss she gets up and goes straight into the house. Normally there is the usual five more minutes before bed, all the sun and running around the garden tonight must have tired her out. I follow Niamh in and head straight up the stairs to run a bath for her before bed.

My alarm clock goes off at the ridiculous time of four am. I creep very slowly out of bed, careful not to wake Shane. Once I get out to the hall, I tiptoe to the bathroom to get a shower. I have already laid out today's clothes last night, so I get myself dried and changed into them. Thankfully, I didn't need to wash my hair, so I just throw it up in a bun.

By the time I'm ready, it's nearly twenty to five in the morning. I lean over and give Shane a kiss and say my goodbyes. He half stirs and mutters something that I don't quite catch. I close our room door once more and walk along the landing to Niamh's room door and pop my head in. Niamh is like a star fish lying on her bed, most of the covers are kicked off on the floor. I pick them up and put them over her, before giving her a tender kiss on the head and quietly sneaking out of her room again and closing the door behind me. The spare room is at the end of the landing where my mum is sleeping. I don't bother popping my head into my mum's room as she is a light sleeper, and I don't want to wake her.

I go downstairs where my case is packed and call a taxi to take me to the airport. I drag my case outside to wait for the taxi, lock the door and post the front door key through the letter box.

I see my taxi pull in round the corner and start to pull my case down the drive.

"Hi, to the airport please," I say while pulling my case into the seven-seater taxi.

"Sure, you off to somewhere nice?"

"I'm off to Sweden. I would love to say it was for leisure, but I will be working so I could be anywhere."

"Sweden, Abba land that will be nice. I hear they have an Abba Museum in Stockholm, and the Mrs. is desperate to go over and see it. She loves Abba."

"Well, it's Stockholm I'm going to for work, so if I get a free couple of hours, I will go to the museum. I like Abba myself."

I still feel a bit tired from getting up so early. After I've made small talk with the driver, I stare out the window but can feel my eyes going together as though I am ready to fall asleep once more. I will need to get a coffee when I get to the airport, hopefully that will wake me up a bit, I think. Just as I'm getting comfy and starting to nod, the taxi man shouts right lass that will be thirty Euros, please.

"Grand. Can you write me a receipt, please? I need a receipt for my expenses at work."

"Aye, sure can," he then leans over onto the passenger side and looks through the drawer and pulls out his receipt book.

"There you go. Have a safe trip."

I take the receipt and put it into the front zip of my purse and shout thank you as I leave.

Once in the front foyer of the airport, I look up to the screens for the departures board and see the Stockholm flight at eight ten am as planned and the check-in desk open. I make my way to the queue and see there are already a few folk waiting to be checked in, so I go and take my place in the line. It moves fast and before I know it, I'm at the front of the line. Almost on autopilot I hand over my passport and lift my case up to be put through check in. Forgetting how heavy it is, I feel a twinge in my back the moment I pull it up. I've never been one for travelling light, I cram everything bar the kitchen sink into my suitcase. Shane and I had to pay before, when we came back from holidays due to me packing so much.

Once I'm all checked in, I look at my watch and it's only twenty to six am, I have loads of time until my flight. I make my way to the food village cafe before security to get a coffee and a pastry. While enjoying my coffee and food I pull out my phone and send a text to my boss.

> Hey that's me at the airport having a coffee. Waiting to go through security will email you tonight. Michelle

I have a scroll through my phone to check my social media accounts and tag myself flying off to Sweden on Facebook. I have a quick scan through my news app and catch up on what's happening in the world. Before long I've a few new notifications on Facebook after tagging myself taking off to Sweden. There are a few likes from family and friends and Sinead has written to have a great time. I scroll down a bit further and see a comment from an old friend Roisin, as I read the comment I laugh aloud.

> SWEDEN! HAVE A BLAST...DON'T RUN INTO ANY OLD FRIENDS OVER THERE. 😉

Shit! I better delete that comment quick before Shane sees it and wonders what's going on. I then send Roisin a private message on messenger asking how she's doing and telling her it's been too long we need to get a catch up sometime and explain why I had to delete her comment. I take the last sip off my coffee and reach over the chair for my handbag before setting off to security. I arrive at security and thankfully at this time of the morning the queue is not so bad, again I take my place in another line and wait my turn.

Once through security, I can finally relax as I browse through the shops while waiting for my flight. Before when I used to travel all the time, if it was after lunch, I would always have a glass or two of wine, kidding on I was sophisticated and civilised, people watching at the airport. Pfftt, I don't know who I was kidding, because by the time the plane would touch down back in Dublin, I was anything but sophisticated and civilised.

I walk about a bit but the sign for Benefit cosmetic catches my eye and I walk over to their stand to try some products. I look for their tinted moisturiser as I could really do with a new one. I try a couple of products and then find one that I like and get that. I stroll a bit more over to the perfumes and try on different perfumes until I decide on my usual choice of Marc Jacob Dot. Once I like something, I can't usually be persuaded to try something else, unless I get a new perfume as a present and the smell grows on me. Once I've checked out the duty free, I go find my gate and sit near to it, waiting to board my flight. I pull out my phone and go on to my iBook account and continue reading the book I have been reading while I wait. After some time, we are finally called to start boarding the plane.

I check my ticket to see what seat I am – 18 A. Great, I love a window seat. Nothing better than watching the ground pull away from underneath me during takeoff and landing. Time passes quickly when I'm up in the air. The stewardess comes round with a snack, and I take water from her. It's a beautiful day for travelling, with blue skies and the odd cloud up high in the sky. I stare out into the abyss of blue sky, while lost in my own thoughts. My thoughts go to Niamh and hope she gets to school okay and make a mental note to call my Ma as soon as I get to the hotel to ensure everything has gone to plan this morning. I think about work and want to get this deal tied up as quickly as possible to get back home and hopefully have a bit of free time to wander around the city and see the sights. An announcement comes over the tannoy that we are preparing to land.

My mind starts wandering again, not to the present but too long ago, when I was young and carefree with no responsibilities and wonder how my life would have turned out if I had continued to see Mattias, would I have moved to Sweden, or would he have moved to Ireland? I think most people have that 'what if' in their life, but life's a funny old thing at the end of the day: what will be, will be. Or as me Ma always says, what's for ya won't go by ya.

Chapter Twenty-One

I get off the plane and follow the herd of people in front of me who have the same thing in mind, grabbing their luggage and getting out as quick as possible. The walk from the plane to the luggage point isn't too long. I see a sign for the toilets. I quickly dash to the loo as the escalator hasn't started going round yet with everyone's luggage. When I come back out from the toilet, I see the carousel has started up. I wait for what feels like forever and finally spy my case, squeezing past the people in front of me, I then grab it and go. I head out to the taxi area to get a taxi into the city. I can't be bothered waiting on buses and checking timetables. I always want the fastest route possible to where I am going. Out in the taxi area, I need not worry as there are endless rows of taxis waiting to take people to where they want to go.

"Hi there, can you take me to The Sheraton hotel please?"

"Yes, no problem. Jump in."

I look around to grab my case, but the taxi driver has kindly picked it up and put it in the boot for me.

I can tell we are getting closer to the city as the congestion gets worse. I check my watch and it's taken almost forty minutes to get from the airport to here.

"Are we nearly there yet?" I ask impatiently.

"We are not far away, maybe another ten minutes," he gives a raise of his hands as if to say *I know, I'm pissed off too, but what can I do?*

I nod my head and smile to give an unspoken gesture that I sympathise with him and know it's not his fault.

The traffic starts moving again, the long straight in the road makes it look like there are thousands of cars in front of us and that we will never get to my destination. I pull out my phone to call me Ma.

"Hey Ma, it's me. How did everything go today? Did Niamh get away okay to school?"

"Hi, love, yeah she was grand, no bother. We were there ten minutes early; I watched her play with her friends till the bell rang and then I left."

"Oh, that's good. Thanks Ma."

"Is that you at your hotel now?"

"No, I'm still in the taxi going to the hotel. The congestion has been a nightmare, we've been stuck in traffic for ages."

"Well give me a phone when you get to your hotel, so I know you've arrived okay."

"Will do Ma, bye the now."

"Bye Chelle."

No sooner had I put down the phone to my Ma, but we rounded the corner, and the taxi pulls into a big grand looking building, which overlooks the harbour. A bellman is standing waiting and on seeing the taxi pull up, he walked over. As I am busy paying the taxi driver, the bellman takes my case out for me and puts it on his trolley. I follow him into the Sheraton. As I walk into the hotel, I notice on the left there is a lounge area with comfy chairs all dotted about at the windows and there is also a nice round bar, then to the right there is a long wide corridor with the reception area. The area has large tiles that are very shiny and appear to be very slippy. *I will need to watch them when I have my work heels on*, I think to myself.

The bellman is already standing waiting for me to check in, I'm assuming he knows what floor to take my luggage to. I go through the motions of checking in before the very polite lady behind the desk gives me my room key and tells me my room is on the ninth floor.

"You're in luck, your room is ready; normally check-in is three o'clock, but we are not too busy, so we can let you in early."

"Thank you so much. I've just travelled from Ireland and got up at silly o'clock in the morning."

When I get upstairs, I give the bellman a tip and say thank you and close the door. Once in my room I have a look around. The bathroom is a good size. I go check the window, hoping to have a view of the harbour, but when I look out, I become somewhat disappointed my room looks out into a garden view and realise the hotel is slightly rounded. *Och well, I can't have it all I suppose*. The bed is enormous, all in white, and I fall back on it and can already tell I am going to get a great sleep, it's so comfy.

I set up my laptop to send a few work emails and to let the client know I've arrived safely and to ensure all is still good for tomorrow's meet and greet. I pull out my phone once more and call Shane. It rings and rings and after the sixth ring, I think he must be busy so leave a voice mail for him, telling him I've arrived safely and to call me when he gets a minute. No sooner had I finished leaving the voice mail, than I called my Ma again.

"Hi Ma, that's me at the hotel now."

"Grand. What's it like?"

"It's beautiful, it's a very grand building that looks onto the harbour and inside looks nice. I'm going to do some work stuff and then go for a walk about. I tried calling Shane but there was no answer, he must be busy, I'm sure he will call me later."

"He was up and out early this morning, he said he's got a lot of work to do today, so he might be back a bit later. I will just make the tea, and he can heat his dinner up when he comes home," she says warmly.

"Och well Ma, thanks very much. I better go and do some work; I shall call you tonight after dinner and speak to Niamh before she goes to bed."

I sit down at the desk in my room and start checking my emails, Steve has sent me my itinerary for the next few days signing off with the caption at the end.

DON'T SAY I'M NOT GOOD TO YOU......YOU HAVE SOME TIME OFF TO EXPLORE THE CITY. ☺

I check my itinerary for my trip. I meet with Mr. Johansson and his associates tomorrow at ten am, spend a few hours with them and then have the rest of my time here free to explore Stockholm. Great, I have Saturday and Sunday all day free to myself. *I will go to the Abba Museum now*, I think to myself.

I reply to Steve telling him he's the best boss and I will keep him up to date with everything over the weekend. I then send an email to Mr. Johansson and his assistant telling them I arrived and put a bit of small talk into the email and sign off by saying I look forward to meeting them all tomorrow.

I go for a shower and freshen up. Once out the shower, I choose to go a walk about Stockholm, now I have the rest of the day to myself. Once outside the hotel, I look to the left and then to the right, to establish where I'm going to go first. Over on the right-hand side I see a very impressive building and start walking over to it to explore. I cross the road and walk round by the harbour and as I get closer to the building, the sheer size of it and its architecture looks amazing. There are beautifully kept green grass garden patches and what looks like a solid gold tomb of a Viking. I walk around and take some pictures. I go to further inspect the impressive building and its grounds and I spy a notice telling me it is Stockholm city hall. As I walk away from the grounds, I follow the path round the water. I walk for some time and have no clue where I'm walking to, just people watching and looking at the impressive buildings as I go. I think I've walked too far and chose to head back to the hotel and ask for directions to get to the shopping district.

I cross the road again and see the back of The Sheraton and hope I can go in the back entrance instead of walking all the way back around. I cut down what can only be described as an alley – it doesn't look as grand as the front of the hotel. I walk about halfway down where I see two doors swing open and two staff members come out. One is wearing a chef uniform and the other is dressed in a smart blue suit. They are chatting to one and other, in what I presume to be Swedish and laughing. I know that laugh, I've heard it before long ago. They start walking towards me, but don't notice me as they are chatting back and forth to each other. I look at the tall man on the left and recognise his frame. He looks away from the other, laughing and then looks dead at me, our eyes meeting. He pulls an expression I don't recognise and suddenly stops.

"Chelle... Michelle, is that you?"

Mattias grins and walks faster over to me. He looks like he's seen a ghost and must come over and ensure he isn't seeing things.

"Mattias, hello you. Long time no see," I lean in and give him a cuddle.

Mattias turns and speaks to the other staff member in Swedish, he answers him back and walks away.

"This is crazy, how are you, Chelle? How have you been?"

"I'm good, thanks. You look well, you've not aged a bit, must be all the Swedish air."

"Oh, thank you," he says with a coy grin. "What are you doing here in Sweden?"

"I'm here on business till Monday and then fly back home. Are you working in The Sheraton?" I ask.

"Yes, I'm the General Manager for the hotel. I have been here for three and a half years now."

"Good. Do you like it?"

"Yes, it's a good company to work for and it's not too far from my house. What about you, what are you up to?"

"I work for an Irish whisky company, we sell to businesses all over the world, so I'm here tying up a deal."

"Woo! That's great," Mattias says nodding as though he's impressed.

There's now a bit of an awkward silence between us both as we stand staring and smiling at each other and the longer we do, the slightly more awkward it gets, not knowing what to say next.

So, I chose to break the silence.

"Are you working late tonight?"

"No. I was on an early, I'm finished at four today and then off for two weeks on holidays," he says with a happy grin.

"Oh, are you going somewhere nice on your holidays?"

"No, I just need to use some of them up. I'm looking forward to doing nothing for two weeks."

"What are you doing tonight?"

The words are out of my mouth before I realise and there seems to be an uncomfortable pause again.

"Nothing planned. What about you?"

"I was going to go and get some dinner and go for a walk."

"Do you want some company? I can show you Stockholm sights," he says with a warm smile.

"Yes, that would be nice. Where and when should I meet you?"

"Do you want to meet at say seven pm at the Hard Rock Cafe? It's in the central part of Stockholm – you could walk it from here but if you don't know where you're going, it's best to take a taxi."

"Grand, will see you then," I say with a smile.

We both awkwardly look at each other for a minute smiling, not sure if we should give each other a goodbye cuddle or just say our goodbyes and leave. Mattias then makes the first move and reaches in to give me a goodbye embrace.

"It was lovely to see you again, Chelle, after all these years. It's a small world, really," he says shaking his head, not believing he's seen an old ghost from long ago.

"Yes, I know, I can't believe I've bumped into you. Bye Mattias, see you tonight," I say smiling.

"See you, Chelle," he says sincerely.

Just like that, he walks away. I stand and watch him, still gob smacked that out of all the millions of people that live in Stockholm, I would bump into him. He turns back around and smiles at me and gives me a wave.

Jesus, Mary, and Joseph I need to call Rochelle and my mum they will never believe who I've just bumped into. I pull out my phone and scroll down till I see Rochelle's name in my contacts and start dialing her.

"Hey, Chelle I'm just at the school waiting on the kids, you alright? I thought you were going to Sweden today?" she asks concerned.

"I'm in feckin Sweden and you are never going to believe who the hell I've just bumped into." Without even finishing my sentence, Rochelle guesses.

"Nooo, no way! Mattias?"

"Yeah. I can't believe it. I was literally just walking back to my hotel."

"What's he like now? Is he still hot?

"He doesn't look like he's changed a bit, he's still hot. He's got the odd wrinkle, but he looks bloody great. I'm going out for dinner tonight with him, but now I'm getting second thoughts. What happens if Shane finds out? I would be so mad if Shane did that to me," I say to Rochelle with a sick feeling in my stomach.

"Sure, now you go out for dinner with him. It's like meeting an old friend you haven't seen for years and catching up on how they are getting on. Shane won't find out and it's not like you're cheating, you're meeting an old friend," she says approvingly, egging me on.

"You sure?"

"Course I am. You better go out for that dinner tonight and I want you to call me tomorrow and tell me everything. Listen I better go, Chelle, that's the kids coming."

"Okay I will then. Speak to you later."

By the time I get back to the front door of the hotel, I realise I've just done a full circle, from meeting Mattias at the back exit to walking right round the building. As I walk through the hotel lobby, I decide I'm not going to tell my Ma, as she would only talk me out of going for dinner with him tonight. I can hear her now saying the past is the past and there's no point dragging it back up into the present. I will tell her tomorrow after I've had dinner with Mattias, then she can't give me the guilt trip.

Chapter Twenty-Two

As the taxi pulls up to the Hard Rock Cafe, I check my watch and it's six fifty-five. I've surprised myself that I got here on time. I didn't think I would get out the door tonight, I had a fashion show for one inside my hotel room. I couldn't choose an outfit, so in the end I opted for dress jeans, heels, a white fitted top and a white and blue blazer. I didn't want to go over the top, as I didn't want Mattias getting the wrong idea, so kept it casual. When I finally decided what I was wearing I phoned home, Niamh told me all about her day and I spoke to my Ma. Shane still wasn't home from work, so I told me Ma a wee white lie, that I was going to bed, as I was tired from all my travelling today and would catch Shane tomorrow.

As I get out of the taxi, I see Mattias vaping, waiting on me. I give him a wave and he flashes a warm smile with a nod of his head. The closer I get he looks at me up and down then smiles once more.

"You look nice."

"Thank you, so do you."

He's also wearing jeans and a nice ice blue shirt that shows his tan. I follow him to the front door, he stands to open the door and gestures for me to go first. Once inside, Mattias speaks to the waiter in Swedish. I haven't a clue what they are saying as I follow them both to a window seat and the waiter hands us some menus. We both study the menu for a bit.

"What do you fancy, Chelle?"

"I think I will get the BBQ cheeseburger and a dirty Martini. What about you?"

"I'm going to get the surf and turf burger."

"Do you not want a cocktail also?" I ask.

"No. I think I will stick to beer," Mattias says with a laugh.

As we order our food we sit and chat about what we have done with our lives for the past seventeen years. I tell him about Niamh, Shane, and my work and how it brought me over here. He tells me he's worked all over the world in different hotels.

"You followed your dreams, then."

"What do you mean?" he asks.

"You once told me you wanted to see the world. So, you did it then. Why did you come back to Stockholm, were you getting fed up traveling the globe?" I ask curiously.

"My mother was getting older and had cancer. She's okay now, thank goodness. I just thought it was best I came home to make sure she was okay. What about your parents, how are they?"

"They're both grand. Thankfully they haven't had any health conditions, I do worry about them especially as they are getting older. I live under three hours away and my Ma, she's staying at mine just now, giving Shane a hand with Niamh, so that's nice she enjoys spending time with her," I explain.

"Do you still like your music, Chelle? Are you still a crazy Spice Girls fan?" he asks with a giggle.

"I do still like my music. I guess it's changed the older I've gotten. I'm loving Adele now; I've hung up my platform trainers and shoes. I guess I'm a bit old now. Talking of music, I see Stockholm has an Abba Museum; I'm hoping to go there on Saturday. Have you ever been? Is it any good?"

"No. I've never been," he says laughing.

"What? Why are you laughing?"

"I might not have seen you in seventeen years, but I'm not surprised you want to go there. You've not changed that much."

"Don't you knock Abba; I love their music."

Just then our food arrives. I felt hungry before I came out, but now seeing the size of the burger, I don't think I will finish it all.

"Anything you can't finish; just give it to me, I won't waste it," Mattias says while patting his stomach.

We chat some more over dinner; he asks after my friends and some of the people he met in Cobh when he worked there. He then asks about Shane and what he does for a living.

"What about you, do you have a special someone in your life?" I ask, intrigued, hoping he does.

Mattias pulls a serious sad face and already I start to feel bad that I asked the question.

"Well, there was someone. She was Australian and her name was Charlotte; I met her in Paris at a bar. We were together for a few years, and we found out she was expecting, I proposed, and we were incredibly happy. Then one day I got the worst call of my life, Charlotte was on her way to work and got hit by a drunk driver killing her and our unborn child. That was five years ago. Not long after that, I found out my mum wasn't well, so I left Paris and came back home. You would have liked her, she was lovely," he says with a distant look on his face.

"That is awful, Mattias. I am so sorry to hear that." I put my hand on top of his for reassurance. I think of Mattias being a father and can't help but think he would have been a great father and husband. Then wonder about the two wee boys I saw on his profile picture.

"Yes. It was terrible at the time. I drank a lot and felt I was in a dark hole that I couldn't get out of. With time it does get easier, but grief always leaves a mark on you. Since then, I've tried to avoid relationships. Anyway, you sound like you have a great life with Shane and Niamh," he says changing the subject.

Mattias' words stick in my mind.

You sound like you have a great life.

For a few moments I drift away in my own thoughts and look out the window. *I do sound like I've got a great life, but looks can be deceiving*, I think to myself.

"Chelle? Chelle."

"Sorry. I was away in a dream there."

Mattias was trying to get my attention as the waiter wanted to take away my plate and wanted to know if I was finished. I order another cocktail, Mattias is still sipping his pint and when asked he doesn't want another beer just yet. After what he's told me, I wonder if alcohol is a trigger for him. I make a conscious thought that my next drink will be a soft drink.

"What else is there nice to do in Stockholm?"

"Lots. You should go to the old town, that's stunning and there are nice restaurants up there."

"How do I get there?"

"As you come out of your hotel, go left, and cross the road then go over the bridge and follow the road around and up. It's maybe a good ten to fifteen minutes from your hotel."

"Thanks. I might go for a walk there tomorrow evening and look for somewhere nice to eat."

"If you walk to the top, you will come to a cobbled street and on the corner, there is a lovely Italian restaurant there, you might like. I'm not doing anything tomorrow, if you don't want to be sitting by yourself, I could join you," he says matter of fact.

"Yes, great. Why not?" I smile.

I get a ping on my phone. I quickly check it as I think it may be Shane. It's not. It's Rochelle, she has sent me a message.

Well, how's your date going? With Mr. Scandanavian? 😊 xx

I give out a laugh after I read it and think I will text her when I get back to the hotel.

"Everything okay? Mattias asks.

"Yes. Everything is fine Rochelle has just sent me a message, trying to be funny that's all."

"Okay," Mattias laughs, as if he knows there is something in the message about him.

I start to giggle, more with embarrassment and can feel my face go red.

We chat some more but I now feel myself starting to get very tired after all the travelling I have done today and check my watch – it's nine fifty. I think I had better head back as I have my meeting tomorrow and need to close this deal.

"Mattias, do you mind if we get the bill? I'm really starting to feel knackered; I was up at silly o'clock this morning and I'm starting to feel exhausted now," I say letting out a yawn.

"Sure. No problem."

Mattias goes and pays the bill. I protest as I want to pay half of it, but he won't let me. We then leave and start walking back.

"Do you want me to call you a cab?"

"No. I was just going to walk back. I love walking through cities at nighttime, people watching and looking at everything lit up."

"I will walk you back then."

"You sure, you don't have to?"

"No. It's fine."

We walk along the streets, looking in shop windows, laughing and chatting as we go.

"You know what surprises me here, Mattias, is the fact that we are not seeing any late-night drunk people staggering along the streets. At this time of night in Dublin, you would have passed quite a few by now."

"It's quite expensive here in Stockholm. A lot of people tend to drink in the house. If people wanted to go out drinking to bars, they wouldn't go out till about ten pm or even later as you couldn't afford to sit and drink in a bar all day here."

I find myself just following Mattias' lead, crossing roads and going to the next street. I have no clue how to get back to the hotel but I'm enjoying the walk, especially after eating that massive burger which could have fed about three people. We finally get back onto a street I recognise from this afternoon and can see The Sheraton in the distance. When we finally get to the front door of the hotel, I turn to Mattias.

"Thank you for a nice night. It was nice to see you again after all these years. If you give me your number, I will send you a text tomorrow to see if you still want to go to the old town tomorrow evening. I will know tomorrow after the meeting what sort of time I will be ready for."

Mattias gives me a warm smile and a flash of his white pearly teeth that don't seem to have lost their brightness in the last seventeen years.

"Yes, it was good to see you again Chelle. Also, you've not changed, you're still the same."

We give each other a hug and then exchange numbers. I walk away with a smile on my face and a spring in my step. I walk through the lobby and press the button to call the lift. When I get to my room, I use my makeup wipes to take off my makeup then check my phone again once more before setting my alarm for tomorrow. I quickly brush my teeth and get straight into bed.

I wake up to the sound of my alarm going off at seven am. I slept like a baby last night. Normally, I take ages to go off to sleep or wake up several times in the night, but that was the best sleep I had in ages. As I reach over to turn my alarm off, I notice I have another message from Rochelle.

Well????

I completely forgot to text Rochelle back last night. *I better message her back now*, I think to myself.

Will call you later. I sat and chatted to him for ages about anything and everything. Meeting him again tonight lol xx

The time quickly passes and after breakfast I check my watch. It's eight thirty am, which means it will be seven thirty back home. I dial Shane.

"Hello Michelle. Sorry I never got a chance to speak to you yesterday, work was crazy. How's Sweden?"

"Yeah, it's fine. I pottered about yesterday and then just had an early night. I've got a meeting at ten with the client that should probably take a couple of hours then I have the rest of the day to myself."

"Nice. You'll be enjoying the peace and quiet."

"Yeah. I am going to go to the Abba Museum at some point while I'm here. What about you, what are your plans for the weekend?"

"Hopefully get finished sharp today then. I'm not sure, will see what your Ma and Niamh are up to."

"You not going to the golf club this weekend?"

There's a small pause on the line.

"Yeah, I might will see what the craic is."

"Is me Ma and Niamh there or have you left already?"

"I left about ten minutes ago. Your Ma was up, Niamh was still sleeping."

"I will maybe give them a phone in a bit, if not will call them when Niamh's back from school. Will let you go the now and talk later. Bye, love you," I say before hanging up

I decide to give my Ma and Niamh a quick call, and after I've spoken to them both, I quickly put on my makeup before I need to get a taxi to my morning meeting. When I spoke to my Ma, I purposely left out the bit of bumping into my old friend.

Chapter Twenty-Three

I stare out of the taxi window and watch the landscape pass by quickly. I can't help thinking something feels off with me today but I'm not sure what. I just can't put my finger on it. I toss back and forth with my own thoughts, wondering am I only thinking this because I had dinner with Mattias last night.

I arrive at my meeting ten minutes early and I go to the front desk.

"Hi, I have a meeting with Mr. Johansson at ten am," I say.

"Yes, can I have your name please?"

"Michelle Doyle."

The receptionist picks up the phone.

"That's fine if you take a seat over there someone will come and get you."

I sit for a few minutes, before a tall, blonde woman shows me through to the office: a middle-aged man is sitting behind his desk in a business suit and tie and he rises to greet me.

"Hello Michelle, nice to finally meet you in person," he reaches out his hand to shake mine.

"Hi, Mr. Johansson, nice to finally meet you in person."

"Please, call me Eric," he gestures for me to take a seat.

"Thank you. Do you have somewhere I can plug my laptop into?" I ask.

"Yes. Of course, give me your cable. Do you want a tea or a coffee?" The blonde asks while taking my charger from me.

"A coffee please milk, no sugar. Thanks."

I start setting up my laptop, and I pull up my powerpoint and notes for my pitch. The blonde comes back with my coffee and now two other males enter the room. Eric introduces the first one as his son and the second as his son-in-law.

I get started on my pitch. I talk about the whisky and our company and the process the whisky goes through to taste so good. I also give them figures on what our sales are in other European countries and talk about trends etc. I take a bottle of our whisky from my bag and pour them all some. I later find out that the blonde named Astrid is married to Eric's son, Alfred. I ask Astrid for some ice to complement the whisky. Once I've done my pitch and they've all had a small shot to warm the hairs on their chest, as my gran used to say, I'm a sitting duck for questions.

"If any of you have any questions, I would be happy to answer," I say confidently.

"The whisky is nice and smooth. What is the difference between blended and Malt whisky?" Eric asks with a smug look on his face. I'm guessing that's him checking to see if I know my facts, as I usually always get asked these questions by men of a certain age.

"Well, sure malt whisky is made from a single type of grain, and the grain is usually grown in a specific region, giving the whisky its distinctive flavour and malt whisky is aged for longer. Whereas blended whisky is a marriage of two types of whisky, made totally separate and then blended," I say with a nod to Eric.

He gives a smile and a nod back at me. I was right, he was just throwing in that grenade question to ensure I knew what I was talking about.

"How much would we sell this to hotel and bar chains?" Alfred asks while looking at the bottle of whisky in his hand.

"If you buy in bulk of us for, say, 160 Kr to one bottle then you can sell to chains for say 200 Kr. We will support you with marketing and after sales as well."

They look at each other and nod then Eric turns to speak to me.

"Michelle, do you want to go and grab yourself another coffee? We will have a chat and then get you back in," he says in a friendly tone, which makes me think he's going to buy from us. I can usually tell at this point which way it's going to go.

"Yes, will do thanks." Astrid then ushers me out into the foyer.

There are a few magazines on the coffee table beside the couch that I'm sitting on, but they are all in Swedish so I take out my phone and send Steve a text.

> Pitch done. I'm sitting outside and they are having a private chat. Keep you posted. Talk soon. Michelle.

No sooner have I sent off the text Steve text back.

> Good, good. Keep me informed. I have every faith in you Michelle. Steve.

Astrid comes back with a coffee for me. I have scroll on Facebook and notice I have a friend request; I click onto it to see who it is and when I see the name I get a small flutter in my stomach. It's from Mattias Karlsson and I quickly accept. I go onto my other social media and have a nosy at that before reading the latest depressing news on the news app. After what seems like ages, they call me back in.

"Michelle we are going to go with your product. For our first order, we shall put in an order of fifty cases and see how that goes and if it sells well, we shall double the order," Eric says with a smile, then rises and holds out his hand once more to secure the deal.

"Great, thank you," I stretch my hand out to meet Eric's.

"I'm just going to send an email off to my boss Steve and let him know. If you don't mind signing some of these papers." I then rummage through my bag to find the paperwork to close the deal.

After all the paperwork is signed and scanned back to my head office, Eric asks if I would like to go for a celebratory lunch with them.

"Yes, why not. That would be nice. Thank you," I reply.

The taxi pulls up outside one of the many restaurants lined in a row. There are tables outside a few of them, looking at the buildings and the streets I can tell this is an affluent neighbourhood. I follow their lead, Eric has obviously been here before, as he strides along the pavement knowing exactly where he's going.

We head on into the middle restaurant called Sture Hof, and as soon as we are in the smell of seafood hits me. I guess Mr. Johansson is feeling like seafood. He stands and talks to the waiter in Swedish, looking at him he gives off a powerful presence of a man who's very sure of himself and confident around others. We all follow the waiter and Eric to be seated.

Time passes quite quickly, and I'm now on my second glass of white wine and I feel it's gone straight to my head. I always get a bit giggly on wine and think to myself I better slow down. There's normal drunk then there is wine drunk, and I'm not going to be unprofessional and get bladdered at a work lunch. I would never do that, but they are actually all very nice and I'm feeling very relaxed in their company.

"So, Michelle, your boss is giving you free time till you catch your flight back on Monday."

"Yes, he's very good to me. I couldn't get a direct flight back till Monday and I didn't want him sending me here, there and everywhere getting back home," I say fondly, thinking it was nice of Steve to do that.

"What are you going to do with the rest of your time here?" Astrid asks while studying her nails.

"I'm going to meet an old friend for dinner tonight, then I am going to go to the Abba Museum tomorrow." I'm careful not to say what sex the old friend is. I don't want any judgement, not that I think they would as they don't know me. I guess I'm more conscious of it than anyone else.

"Oh, you like Abba? I've been to the Abba Museum, you will love it," she says nudging Alfred; by the way she's nudging him, I'm certain they went together. I finally get Astrid's attention now; she can't be much older than me. If I were to hedge a bet, I would say early forties.

"Can you sing Michelle, most people from Ireland are great singers. I loved Boyzone when I was a teenager," she says laughing.

"God no, I'm tone deaf. Yeah, Boyzone were good," I then proceed to sing 'No Matter What' by Boyzone and Astrid joins in laughing.

"How much wine have you two had?" Alfred asks jokingly.

The afternoon goes by quickly. I talk back and forth to the three of them, everything from politics to places we would like to visit; they appear to be very warm and friendly people, once business is out the way. In the past when I went travelling before some weren't so nice, but I'm pleasantly surprised I have enjoyed my afternoon with them all, I've surprised myself. I thought it was going to be one of those boring lunches. After my second wine, I think it is a wise idea to drink water, as the wine was going down too well.

"I'm going to head back to my hotel now, I've had a lovely afternoon and thank you again for the business on behalf of the company," I say with a warm smile.

The three of them rise to say their goodbyes and to shake my hand once more.

"Can I order you a cab, Michelle?" Eric says with a concerned tone.

"Nah, I'm grand thanks. I'm going to walk and look around this beautiful city, but thank you."

"Okay. I will email you next week when you're back in the office," he says.

"Thanks Eric, look forward to it."

As I walk out the hotel's main door, Mattias is waiting for me, talking to the porter.

"Hello, how are you?"

"Good, thanks, you?"

"Grand. I felt a bit groggy earlier I went for a nap. I had two glasses of wine at lunch time, and I thought I better go for a sleep," I say with a laugh.

I follow Mattias to cross the road and he stops me with his arm not to go any further until the green light comes on to go. Given the circumstances of what happened, I can understand why he's now cautious. We then proceed to cross the road and up over to the bridge. When I get on the bridge, I stop to take photos of the hotel and the grand city hall, which looks magnificent the way the light of the sun is catching the top of the building in the background.

"Do you want me to take a photo of you?" Mattias asks.

"Yes please," I reply while handing my phone over to him.

I stand with my back to the bridge, with the water and city hall in the distance. Mattias then hands my phone back to me and we carry on. We follow the road round and again there is more water near this time to the left of us as we head on up to the old town. We walk a good fifteen minutes until we finally get there. I feel so relieved, I should never have worn heels.

"Please tell me next time if there's going to be loads of walking and I will not wear these shoes," I say, trying not to show the pain I'm in. All in the name of vanity or fashion. Mattias smiles.

When we get into the restaurant, it's right on the corner and there is a little hill going down the way. It's not an overly big restaurant; it feels quite intimate and homely. There are lots of photos on the walls with famous faces and the table clothes are very old Italy, with red and white squares on them. You can smell all the aromas of Italian food cooking and if you weren't hungry before you came, you certainly will be feeling hungry with the beautiful smells coming from the kitchen. I order bruschetta to start and lasagna as my main, Mattias orders buffalo mozzarella to start and carbonara as his main. We ask for some water for the table and a bottle of red wine.

"How did your meeting go today?"

"It went well, I closed the deal. What about you, what did you get up to today?"

"I had a long lie, for once. Got up later and went over to see my mum and one of my brothers were over with their family also, it was a nice day."

"Oh, that's nice. Is your mum totally fine now?"

"Yes. She's good. She just goes yearly for a check. My

brother took his two boys over, they are eight and five and they are hilarious," he says with a warm smile.

Ah, they must be the two boys I saw in the picture, I think to myself.

After dinner we sit chatting some more while finishing our wine. I receive a text from Shane.

> Hey, hope your meeting went well. I'm just heading out to the golf club for a few drinks. Yer Ma and Niamh are fine, she's playing with yer Ma's hair. Will give you a call tomorrow. Night love you xx

I instantly feel bad and make my excuses to leave the restaurant for a few minutes to call Shane.

"Hey, I just got your text. Sorry I fell asleep a bit earlier. I'm just out having dinner," I say with a horrible feeling in my stomach. I don't like telling Shane lies.

"Oh, you're alright, I knew you would be busy," he says.

"Are you still in the house?" I ask as I can hear Niamh's voice in the background.

"Yes, I'm just leaving in a minute. Will put her on."

"Hi Ma, I miss you."

"Hi chicken, I miss you too. Only three more sleeps then I will be home."

"Yeah, I can't wait."

Shane then comes back on the phone to tell me Niamh is away again to see my Ma.

"Okay, will call you tomorrow. Night, love you," I say, feeling a stabbing pain in my stomach again, thinking what a terrible person I am. I try and push it to the back of my mind and tell myself what Rochelle said the other day: Mattias is just an old friend.

The hairs on my arms are standing up, there is a slight chill in the air now as the night is getting darker and the temperatures dropping.

"Is everything okay?" Mattias asks, concerned.

"Yes, everything is fine. I just needed to speak to Niamh before she went to bed."

"She will be missing you," he says softly.

"Yes. I stopped going on trips when she was born. I only came on this one because the girl who was supposed to go was off sick."

"Ah, so it was fate then," he says smiling.

"What was fate?" I ask not fulling listening to what Mattias is saying. I'm still feeling guilty for going to dinner with my ex and what a terrible person that makes me.

"This," he points at the two of us and laughs.

I pause for a bit, thinking about what he just said.

"Maybe. Me Ma always says everything happens for a reason."

After a while, we get the bill and head outside.

"Where to now? Where would you like to go, Chelle?"

"I'm easy, I'm the tourist; you decide."

"Okay, follow me," he says pointing further down the road.

We go a wander round the old town looking at buildings and all the grand designs. I like Stockholm. It's a beautiful city, steeped in lots of history and architecture. Suddenly my feet start throbbing again.

"Mattias, my feet are getting painfully sore. I think I need to get a taxi. Next time, I will take other shoes," I say trying not to curse under my breath.

"Okay, I will call a cab. Where would you like to go?" he turns to ask.

"I don't mind."

"Do you want to come to mine?" he says with a look I can't quite read.

There is an awkward pause.

Mattias proceeds to say something funny, I don't quite catch.

"I will show you my flat, it's not too far from The Sheraton," Mattias says while looking down at my feet. I think he can tell I'm in agony.

I agree, and Mattias calls a cab. When we arrive at Mattias' place, it is a big sandstone building, he uses his key and lets us both in. We go up the first flight of stairs, which are quite narrow in the corners and then around the second flight of stairs. After climbing the second flight of stairs, I feel knackered and take my shoes off. As soon as I do, I feel the throbbing instantly going away.

"It's okay, we are here now," Mattias says. Then he goes to the door on the right and opens it with his key.

"Thank goodness. I don't think my poor feet could have climbed any more steps," I say with a laugh.

Once inside the hallway it's not too long, but quite wide. It's neutral with a long runner of a carpet and underneath it there is lovely varnished wooden flooring. We walk down to the furthest away door and enter the living room: it's very nice and all completely painted white. There are some paintings on the wall and some photos, and there is a couch and an armchair over in the corner there is a tv and stand. Then, towards the window, there is a small table and chairs. Mattias puts his keys on the table then leaves the living room, and goes into his kitchen. It's a small kitchen but compact, everything looks like it has a specific place in the kitchen.

"Would you like a drink?" he asks.

"What do you have?" I say, trying to look over his shoulder to see into his fridge.

"I have beer, white wine or rose wine?"

"Can I please have a rose?" I ask.

Mattias then pours me wine from the fridge and gets himself a beer. There is a door in his kitchen he opens and there is a small veranda outside the door with a table and chairs.

"You have a lovely home. I bet it's nice sitting out here when the sun is setting," I say while looking out over his veranda at the view.

"Yes, it's nice, but to tell you the truth I don't sit out here that often."

"Are you busy tomorrow?"

"No. I don't think so. Why?"

"Well. If the Abba Museum doesn't bore you too much, do you want to come with me?"

"Yes, why not," Mattias smiles.

"Can I have a look round your flat?"

"Yes, certainly." He stands up and leads the way.

He opens the door to his bathroom: it's tiled wall to floor all white with a stone effect break in the middle. There is a small window on the right-hand side. A large bath to the left with an over-the-top shower and a fancy hand basin in the middle, the bathroom is a good size. Next, we move back into the living room and I have a closer look at the pictures. There is a nice painting of a sunset, it takes up most of the back wall, there are also a few other pictures on the smaller wall, one of Mattias and who I think could have been Charlotte. It's a black and white photo.

Mattias catches me looking. "That was me and Charlotte in happier times in Paris," he says sadly.

"It's a lovely photo, you look very happy. She's very pretty," I say sincerely.

I look at the other photos of Mattias and his family, brothers and sisters. There is also one of Mattias and two young boys, the same photo that he uses for his Facebook profile picture.

"Who are they?" I ask, wanting to put my curiosity at bay.

"These two cheeky little people are my nephews. Hugo and Lucas," he says fondly holding up the picture.

"They are very cute. The elder one on the left looks really like you," I say turning round to look at Mattias.

"Yes, lots of people say Lucas looks very like me. He's my younger brother's son, but I think he looks more like my brother. They are both great kids."

Finally, we go into his bedroom again, it's white, and I can't decide if the house looks too clinical or just in need of a woman's touch.

"You like white, Mattias."

He looks at me, confused. "What do you mean?"

"Every room we have gone into is white."

"When I bought the flat, I couldn't be bothered picking lots of colours, so I just painted the house white," he says with a laugh and shrugs his shoulders.

I walk over to the french doors at the other side of the room in the bedroom and open them, you can go out the balcony here and then walk back in the kitchen way.

"You actually have quite a big balcony."

Mattias doesn't respond to me, he looks for something in his fitted wardrobes and then pulls out a big box.

"I want to show you something," he says excitedly.

I follow Mattias out to the balcony and he puts the box on top of the table. I sit back down and have another sip of my wine wondering what he is going to show me. He opens the box and it is all old photos; we go through a few of them. There is some of Mattias when he was little.

"Aw you were a such a cute wee boy, what happened?" I ask jokingly.

He goes through the box some more and he pulls out another few photos, of me and him. There is one of us at

Blarney Castle, another one of me and him talking in a pub and the last one is of me, him and a few of the other summer staff that worked with us back then and Rochelle, Roisin, and Cara. Looking at the photo, it looks like another lifetime ago. We all look so young.

"Did you ever keep in touch with any of the summer staff?" I ask.

"No. I never kept in touch with any of them. It was different back then, you didn't have social media or anything; nowadays it's a lot easier."

"Yeah. You're right. Look how young we all are and skinny. I'm so thin in that photo, I don't think I will ever be that size again."

"You look fine to me, Michelle," he looks up and our eyes catch and meet. There is a short silence, and I turn to break away eye contact.

"So, let's see what other photos you have here," I say changing the subject quickly and trying not to give Mattias anymore eye contact. I start looking through the box again.

Mattias gets up to get himself another beer from the fridge. He takes the bottle of wine out also and tops up my glass too.

"Will I put on some music?"

"Yes, why not."

"What do you want on. Please don't say Abba," he says laughing.

"I don't mind; surprise me."

Mattias connects his phone to the small blue tooth speaker in the kitchen. The next thing Coldplay – 'Viva la Vida' is playing out the speaker.

"Good choice. I like Coldplay."

"Yeah, they are a good band."

We chat some more; he asks me some more questions about my work and Ireland, and I ask him the same and if he will get itchy feet again and do some more travelling, but he seems to be happy being closer to home now that he is older. I feel a little drunk and the time has just run away with us.

"I should be getting back to the hotel now, it's getting late," I say looking at my watch.

"I will call you a cab."

"No. It's fine. I want to walk as I feel a bit drunk."

"I will walk you back then."

Chapter Twenty-Four

I wake up with a slight hangover and thirst in the morning, my head feeling fuzzy. I have a large bottle of water beside my bed, which I reach over to get a drink out of. I'm supposed to be meeting Mattias later today. I get up to go for a shower. I still feel a bit groggy from last night and I can't be bothered going downstairs for breakfast today, so I choose to call room service and get breakfast brought up.

Once out of the shower and organised, I call home to see what is happening back with the three of them. The phone keeps ringing and ringing, until finally I hear a familiar voice answering the call.

"Hey Ma, how are you all?"

"Oh, hello love," there then appears to be a silence on the line.

"You alright, Ma?"

"Yes, yes. Grand."

"You don't seem yourself. Is everything okay?"

"Aye. Everything's fine," she says, snappy.

"Where's Niamh and Shane. What are you all up to today?"

"Niamh is in there watching the telly. We are going to go to the park and maybe to the cinema later," she says flatly.

"Oh, that will be nice. Niamh will enjoy that," I say warmly.

"What about Shane, is he about?"

There's a long pause on the phone again before she responds.

"Aye, he's away to the dealership, he said he had some stuff to do," she says while letting out a sigh.

"Oh, right, that's not like him to go to the dealership on a Saturday. Can I speak to Niamh please?" I ask curiously, knowing that if there are any secrets, Niamh will blurt them straight out.

"Yeah, I will give her a shout. Speak to you later, love," she says with her voice now changing to a loving tone that I recognise.

"Bye Ma."

"Hi Mammy, I miss you," Niamh says excitedly.

"Hi sweetie, I miss you, too. Not long now until I'm back. Nana said she's taking you to the park and cinema today. That will be fun."

"Yes, I can't wait."

"How was school yesterday?" I ask.

"It was good. Nana shouted at Daddy today," Niamh blurts out.

"What? Why?"

"I don't know."

"Can you put Nana on please, Niamh," I ask, worried.

"Yes, bye Mammy."

I hear Niamh shout to me Ma that I want to talk to her.

"Hi, it's me again. What did Niamh mean by you were shouting at Shane? What's going on, Ma?"

I can hear my Ma sigh. "I wasn't shouting at him; Niamh got the wrong end of the stick."

"Oh, okay. So, what happened?" I ask, concerned.

"I've just not been feeling myself and I can't remember why, but I snapped at Shane," she says, again letting out another sigh.

"You alright, Ma? It's not serious or anything to worry about, is it?"

"No, I'm grand, I've just not been feeling myself."

"So, you and Shane are fine?"

"Yes, of course," she says quietly.

"Okay. I will go just now and leave you and Niamh to get ready. Bye Ma."

"Bye, love."

I hit the call off but can't help feeling my Ma's not telling me the whole truth; something doesn't seem right to me. I've never known my Ma to shout at anyone, let alone my fiancé. I ponder with my thoughts for a few minutes and then pick up the phone again, to call Shane and see what he says about it all.

Just then, I get a knock at the door that must be room service. I can smell the waft of cooked breakfast just before I open the door, I should by now know that familiar smell all too well. Nothing sorts my hangover better than a home-cooked, hearty breakfast. I open the door for the waiter to come in, I feel like I'm doing it on auto pilot, I would normally make small talk but today, I'm not sure if it's my hangover or what Niamh has just told me about my Ma and Shane, but I can't really be bothered talking. I hand a tip over and say thanks and watch the waiter walk out the door. I pour myself a black coffee and lift back the cover and there on the plate, perfectly placed and looking cooked to perfection is toast, two bits of bacon and two poached eggs. I start off well, I almost finish my food, but I'm now just pushing my food around the plate and can't force myself to eat much more. I look at the plate and think I didn't do too bad; I've only left half an egg.

I need to speak to Shane; otherwise my thoughts are going to be of home if I don't.

The phone rings several times before he finally answers.

"Hi Michelle," he says in a serious tone.

"Hi, how's things?"

"Aye, grand," he says with a slight stutter.

"Where are you? All I can hear is the wind blowing down the phone?"

"Eh, I'm at the golf course."

"Oh, right. Ma said you were at the dealership. I thought it was strange you were in on a Saturday," I ask, trying to dig for more information.

"I just popped in for two minutes to send an email and then decided to go to the golf course and have a game. Yer Ma has stuff planned for her and Niamh today." His voice has changed back to the full of the confidence tone I've come to know.

"Oh, right, I see. How's Ma been, is she doing your head in yet?" I say with a laugh but also a suggested tone to see what he says.

"Yer Ma is yer Ma. She's been grand with Niamh. Nah, she's been fine."

"Oh right. Well, I will leave you to your golf and give you a call later."

"Bye Michelle."

I feel a bit better now that I've spoken to Shane. If it was anything too serious I'm sure he would have mentioned it, and I didn't want to mention it to him as I'm so far away. I go and start getting ready, as Mattias will be here soon.

I decide to wear white fitted jeans and a nice camel coloured top. I think about wearing heels but after the other evening I choose against the heels, I want to be comfortable today as I'm sure there will be a lot of walking and I don't want to be in agony. I wear my nice white Nike trainers that I have packed and grab a light blue, short denim jacket.

As I make my way out the front doors, there like clockwork is Mattias, waiting for me.

"Hey, how was your head today?" I ask.

"Fine. Why, did you have a sore head, Chelle? It's a beautiful day. We will walk to the museum if you want?" Mattias suggests while looking up at the sky.

Mattias is right, it is a gorgeous day. The sun is out high in the sky and there isn't one cloud to be seen, there is no wind either. I'm now regretting taking my denim jacket, but I suppose it's light so I can just put over my arm.

"How far is the museum from here?" I ask before committing to walking a great distance.

"It's about a thirty-minute walk."

"Can we grab a taxi and walk back?" I protest.

"Okay," he says with a smile.

Mattias goes and speaks to the door man, I presume he's asking him to order us a cab. After a few minutes, the taxi pulls up. Mattias tells the driver where we are off to and before long, we arrive at the museum.

As I get out the car, the first thing to strike me at the museum is the Abba cut outs at the front door, there are a few people standing waiting to get their photo taken. I watch a group of friends laughing as they stand and put their heads on top of the cut outs and get their photos taken.

"Let's do that." I point over to the cut outs of the four Abba figures.

"Okay, which one are you going to be?" Mattias asks with a laugh.

"I want to be the blonde one, what was her name again?"

"Agnetha, and I think the one with the brown hair was called Anni-Frid."

We walk over to the small line that is now forming and wait patiently to get our photo taken. A gent in the line asks if we want him to take our pictures. I hand my phone and Mattias hands his phone over also. Once taken, the man then hands us back our phones, I look at the picture. I'm laughing and looking at the camera. Mattias is smiling and looking at me.

We walk through to admissions to pay. I take out my purse to pay but Mattias gets there first and pays.

"Thank you. I'm getting lunch though and I won't take no for an answer," I say firmly.

"Okay, you can get lunch," he says with a smile.

We walk through to the museum, which is quite dark, and the first thing to strike me is the Abba logo all lit up in lights. I pull out my camera to take a photo. We walk around some more and see actual clothes they wore on stage and read about their lives and music. We see one of their original cars and a replica of a helicopter that was in one of their music videos. I go sit in the helicopter and Mattias takes a photo of me. There's also a mini studio inside the museum and there are guitars hanging up as well as drums.

We walk round another corner and come across a karaoke room. I pull Mattias into it when others walk out, despite Mattias protesting about not wanting to go in, he eventually gives in and comes into the booth with me. Next song up is Dancing Queen the words start appearing on the screen and we both start singing them, we are laughing and trying to keep in time with the words and music, but it doesn't seem to be going very well. Next song up is Honey, Honey.

"I used to love this song," I shout to Mattias over the music.

Again, we both start singing this time, however we appear

more in time with the music. We finally come out the booth laughing about our music skills.

"I don't think either of us should give up our day jobs to be singers, Mattias. What do you think?"

"No, definitely not," he says with smile.

After I take a few more photos, we head out of the museum and decide to take a stroll by the water.

"I like this part of Stockholm. If we just follow the water's edge around a bit, we will eventually come to the road," Mattias says, while admiring the yachts tied up.

You can tell this part of the city is well-maintained. There's some lovely expensive boats and yachts to the left. The walkway right around the water is all decking. Far ahead you can see lavish buildings, which I think is where the road is at. We walk round the water's edge for a bit, and I stop to take some photos. I take a photo of Mattias with the yachts and water in the background.

Chapter Twenty-Five

"You don't seem yourself today, Chelle, are you okay?"

"Yes, I'm grand. What makes you think that?" I ask, puzzled. How can he tell that my mind is going round in circles every so often, wondering why my mother behaved the way she did this morning.

"I'm not sure. You seem a little quiet, maybe distant," he says, staring dead at me.

"Honestly, I'm fine," I say with a smile.

It's funny how, after all these years, Mattias knows me so well. Maybe he's just very good at reading people's body language; you get people like that, they can just tell if something is off or up with a person.

We finally get to the road and walk up to the traffic lights to cross. I'm enjoying the walk around Stockholm. It's such a beautiful and clean city. Just as I'm admiring the buildings, Mattias pulls me by the arm to cross the road. I was too busy looking everywhere but the traffic lights. We walk some more, and I have a nosey in some shop windows. We have walked at least two miles, not that I'm moaning as the weather is lovely and I'm enjoying Mattias company.

"Oh, I recognise this place, over there is where I went for lunch yesterday with the client," I point, feeling quite chuffed with myself.

"That's a posh place," Mattias says with a raise of his eyebrows.

"I thought it was quite nice."

"Yes, I'm sure," he says in agreement.

We pick a place near to it and sit out to admire the sun and get a drink.

"I'm getting this. Are you hungry?" I say with a serious tone.

"No, I will just have a beer just now. What about you?"

"I think I will just get a wine. I'm not too hungry either."

We order our drinks and sit people watching while we are waiting for them to arrive. I go into my bag and take out my sunglasses as the sun is bright in the sky and every time Mattias is talking to me, I feel like I'm squinting my face to look at him.

"That's better. I can see you now," I say with a laugh.

The waiter comes over with our drinks. The nice, cool glass of rose wine goes down a treat. I'm unaware that I'm sitting starring into space, lost in my own thoughts. Today with my mum and Shane, I just can't shake the feeling off that something doesn't feel right.

"Hello, earth to Chelle," Mattias says with a laugh.

"Oh, I'm sorry I was miles away there," I say finding myself coming back to the here and now.

"What's wrong, Chelle? There is something bothering you, talk to me, let me help you," he says, concerned.

"You can't. I don't know. It's my Ma and Shane, I think they had an argument or something, I'm not sure what, but it's put me wrong ever since I heard about it. I feel like something is off with the whole situation. It's not like me Ma to ever get angry."

"Did your mum tell you? Or did your boyfriend say? How did you find out?"

"My daughter told me when I phoned home this morning and me Ma, she just tried to play the whole thing down. Shane didn't even really mention it, but he seemed off. I'm not sure maybe, I'm looking into it too much."

"Your Ma always seemed nice to me, but I guess that was a long time ago. She's older now, you know what older women can be like. Maybe she's a bit grumpy now."

"Nah, me Ma is always pretty chilled. Och who knows, I guess I will find out when I go back home, I need to stop worrying about it. I can't do anything now."

"You're right," he says lifting his glass to mine.

Mattias receives a call to his mobile, he greets the caller with a warm smile on his face and chats in Swedish. He appears to chat fast, judging by his manner the person on the other end of the line appears to be very familiar to him. I watch him through my sunglasses. There's a slight breeze in the heat and Mattias' thick hair blows about, he has quite a head of hair on him. All Scandinavian men seem to have great hair, I find myself wondering why that is. Mattias hangs up and then informs me it was his older sister, Annika.

"She wants to meet you. She heard everything about you many years ago and she said she wants to meet the famous Irish Michelle."

"Grand, that will be nice. When?"

"She's asked if we want to go over to hers?"

"Yeah, sure why not."

Just then my phone pings, it's a text from Shane.

Hey I'm just texting to say how much I love you, Michelle. I know I take you for granted but I never want to lose you. Missing you, can't wait till your home, love you xx

Dear god, have I just read that text right. Is he drunk? Shane never sends me texts like this. Maybe at the start of our relationship, but not nowadays in the last couple of years; sometimes, I've felt we were two strangers. What's got into him, maybe absence does make the heart grow fonder? I text back.

I love you too. Can't wait to see you both when I'm back. Are you drunk? Xx

No sooner have I hit send, I get another back.

No, it's too early in the day. I just wanted you to know how much I love you and don't know what I would do without you xx

I look at his text on the screen. *If he's not drunk, what the hell has got into him?* I think to myself.

"Everything okay, Chelle?"

"Yeah, just got a text from home. Nothing to worry about, after all. Everything is grand."

I pay our bill and then we go in search of the nearest off licence to take some drinks to Mattias sister's place. I stop at a small supermarket and buy his sister some flowers and chocolates to take with me, before walking for a bit to hail down the first taxi we can find. We get in the taxi and Mattias gives the driver his sister's address. We take a few turns and I have no clue where we are going to, I'm just enjoying looking out the window. It looks like we are leaving the city, as the roads aren't so congested.

We finally get to Mattias' sister house after about thirty

minutes in the taxi, before Mattias can hand over the money I automatically pay the driver. Once out the taxi, there in front of me is a lovely white bungalow, there is a small path with steps going up to the main door and lots of green grass.

As we walk up the path, the front door opens and a middle-aged woman greets Mattias, I presume it's his sister Annika. There are a few striking similarities, she's tall and thin like Mattias and has dark blonde hair. Mattias gives her a warm welcome cuddle.

"Annika, this is Chelle from Cobh," Mattias says very proudly.

"Hi Annika, really nice to meet you," I go to put out my hand, but Annika pulls me into give me a hug.

"Lovely to meet you, Chelle. I heard lots about you many years ago and finally I get to meet you," she says with a warm smile on her face.

We walk through her hall down into her living room. It's beautiful with a lovely leather suede corner couch to the left and a grand fireplace on the centre wall. There are lovely big French doors leading onto the garden.

"These are for you," I say and hand Annika the flowers, chocolate, and wine.

"Thank you, that's very kind of you. Come take a seat," she points for us to sit.

Just then, a teenage girl comes in and Mattias gets up to greet her. He gives her a cuddle.

"Chelle this is my niece – Cecillia," She turns and gives me a shy smile.

"Hello there, nice to meet you," I put my hand out and the young girl shakes it. She must be about fourteen or fifteen.

"How many children do you have, Annika?" I ask.

"I have three. Two boys and one daughter. My boys are out today. It's just me and Cecillia."

"You're very pretty," I say turning to make eye contact with Cecillia.

"Can I get you both something?" Annika asks.

"Can I have a white coffee, please?" I say before sitting back down.

"I will have the same as Michelle."

Annika comes back a bit later and gives us both our coffees.

"If you both want to stay for some food, I am making Falukorv."

"Christ, what is that?" I ask intrigued.

"It's like Irish sausage and mash," Mattias says before Annika can speak.

"Yes, thank you that would be lovely," I say.

The afternoon passes quickly and I chat away to Annika. I learn she is just recently divorced and that she is a nurse, she is an Abba fan also and has been to the museum many times with her friends. I can tell Mattias and his sister are close. He has a big family and I get the impression they are all very close, which I think is very nice. I help Annika set the table – Mattias, always the perfectionist, is finishing off in the kitchen for his sister. He had a taste, and it wasn't up to his standard, so he said he was going to doctor it.

Every so often today I've been getting an uneasy feeling in my stomach, and I've got it again. I can't decide if it's because I'm halfway around the world having dinner with an old boyfriend and his family and I feel guilty as hell, although I haven't done anything wrong, in my heart I know it's wrong. Or is it because what Niamh said to me earlier about my Ma shouting at Shane and then to top it off there's the bloody text that Shane sent to me. Maybe it's all three things that are putting me wrong today.

"Can I use your bathroom please, Annika?"

"Yes of course, it's straight down the hall on the left," Annika says.

I go into the bathroom and sit for a minute to clear my head, I would normally splash my face with water, but I don't want to do that, as I have my war paint on today. I pull out my phone and text Rochelle.

> Hey, got loads to tell you. If I'm back early tonight will call you, if not call you tomorrow. P.S don't call me back the now, as I'm having dinner with Mattias and his sister xx

I head back through to the lounge, and Mattias is plating up the food.

"Do you want a drink, Michelle?" Annika asks while holding up the bottle of rose wine I brought in earlier.

"Yes, please."

I look at the food on my plate and it does look like sausage and mash only fancier, it has some garden peas too. The sausage goes around the plate and the peas are in the middle. I try a bit and I'm instantly impressed.

"Hmm, this is lovely," I say while picking up my wine glass to wash down my food with.

We talk some more about Southern Ireland and Northern Ireland how one state is going to be in the Euros and the other isn't. I tell them about Niamh and how she likes her dance classes, I tell them she does traditional Irish dancing. Mattias opens another bottle of wine and tops up our three glasses. I help Annika clear the dishes from the table.

"No Michelle, please put them down, you are a guest in my home," Annika says firmly.

"Honestly, Annika I want to help. You have been so kind, inviting me to your lovely home and feeding me, it's the least I can do," I start walking through to the kitchen with the plates.

Once I help Annika get tidied up, I sit back down on the couch with Mattias to finish my wine.

"What are you wanting to do after this, Chelle?" Mattias asks, turning to face me.

"I've had a nice day. The Abba Museum was craic. I think I might head back to the hotel. What about you?"

"I will take you back. You're not wanting to go clubbing then?" Mattias asks, laughing.

"No. I think I'm starting to show my age now," I say with a smile.

Mattias pulls out his phone and calls a taxi. After a while, the taxi arrives, we both say our goodbyes to Annika. I thank her for her hospitality and hope that maybe we might meet again someday. She is such a lovely lady, very warm and friendly, I remark to Mattias. The taxi pulls back up at The Sheraton.

"Are you sure you want to go back just now, there is a nice bar just around the corner, we could have a night cap before you go back to your hotel?"

"Och why not. You've twisted my arm. Not that it needs much twisting," I say laughing.

Just then, I go over my ankle slightly. Mattias catches me.

"Are you drunk, Chelle?" Mattias asks while holding out his arm for me to hold on to.

"Maybe slightly," I say giggling.

I automatically take Mattias' arm and link my arm with his. After a few steps walking, I feel a bit funny linking his arm, but I keep linking his arm anyway and then push the thought to the back of my mind.

Mattias stops for a minute and turns to look me in the eyes. "I'm glad I bumped into you the other day, I often wondered about you over the years, what became of you. If you were married and happy."

"I thought about you also from time to time and then I

would try to push you to the back of my mind," I say very matter of fact.

He looks at me with a horrified look on his face. "Why?"

"When I realised we would probably never see each other again, I felt heartbroken and I thought it was easier to forget. You were my first love. Although I am glad, Mattias, that we bumped into each other too. It's been so nice to see you again after all these years," I say with a warm smile.

"I'm telling you, it's fate," he says while brushing a bit of hair out of my face.

I can feel the connection and tension between us, but I have a life back home and I pull away from Mattias' embrace, knowing that, if I stay looking too long at this man, I may do something I later regret. I need to step back into my own space and keep a distance between us. I also want him to step back into his.

"Mattias, I like you a lot. I think you know that, but I have Shane and Niamh back home. I can't do that to them," I say softly, not wanting to hurt Mattias' feelings, but also being conscious not to lead him on and feel it needs to be said.

"I know, I'm sorry." He lifts my hand up and gently kisses the back of my hand. "Shane is a lucky man. I hope he knows that," he says lifting his eyes to catch mine ones more.

I hope he knows that, too, I think to myself.

We carry on walking to the bar and there is no awkward silence or anything, we both said what we felt, and I feel it's cleared the air now. I think to myself, what will happen when I go home, will I ever see him again? Will we keep in touch? I can't imagine Mattias ever coming to visit, I'm not sure how that would go down with Shane. Us all sitting around the table, playing at happy friends with my fiancé and my ex-boyfriend from years ago. Who I still appear to have feelings for, or maybe it's just warmth like a deep friend thing or something, I don't know, I'm not a relationship guru, I'm terrible for over thinking things and analysing in my head, the stress I give myself.

We go into the bar and there are a few folks in, but it's not overly busy, outside its dusk and after what Mattias said the other day about bars not getting busy until late, I can tell it's still very early. We sit by the window and Mattias goes and orders us two drinks.

"So, what are the plans for tomorrow. It's my last day," I say pulling a sad face.

"What do you fancy doing tomorrow?"

"I wouldn't mind doing a bit of shopping. I promised Niamh I would get her something."

"No problem. I will take you to the shopping district tomorrow. They close a bit earlier with it being Sunday, I can pick you up again about lunchtime tomorrow, if you want?"

"Grand, sounds like a plan," I say raising my glass up to Mattias'.

"What time is your plane on Monday?"

"I think I leave about nine am. So I will probably be at the airport for about seven."

I pull out my phone and I see a few messages from Rochelle.

"Rochelle has been texting me. Sit beside me and I will send her a picture of us both."

We sit beside each other holding up a glass of wine each, smiling into the camera. I hit send. Within seconds of me sending it, I see a message back from Rochelle.

Great photo. Tell big sexy he's still got it 😊 xx

I let out a laugh and repeat the text to Mattias, who also

starts laughing now. We sit chatting and laughing for quite a bit, as the time quickly passes by. Mattias asks if I want another drink, I say no, as I feel I've had enough for one day.

We decide to call it a night, and Mattias walks me over to my hotel once more. We say our goodbyes and give each other a warm hug good night.

Chapter Twenty-Six

Once back up in the hotel room I call Rochelle and fill her in with the last few days with Mattias and what happened tonight.

"Did he really say that? He's still carrying a flame for you, Michelle, after all these years," she says quickly. Knowing Rochelle, when she talks in a fast tone she's getting carried away and excited and doesn't let go of something.

"I think it was the wine talking. We had a bit to drink today at his sister's house. I stopped it before it went any further." I say seriously.

"I bet you that wee devil on your shoulder was telling you to go for it," she says with the dirtiest of laughs.

Her dirty laugh always makes me laugh. Even when we were kids, Rochelle's laugh was always funnier than the joke and whenever she started laughing, I would start.

"Well, I did think twice but the angel won. As my old Nana would say, keep your hand on yer ha'penny, and I certainly did," I say jokingly and we both laugh some more.

We say our goodbyes and I tell her I will call her next week when I'm back in Ireland.

Mattias takes me to a nice shopping centre not far from my hotel. I buy Niamh an Elsa doll from the Disney film Frozen and a cute Olaf teddy, I know she will like them both. We wander into a food and gifts shop and I get my parents some Swedish cookies.

"You know the name for the Swedish cookies is quite a mouthful. I will pay to hear your parents try to pronounce them," Mattias remarks. "It's pronounced Nyakers Pepparkakor."

"Jesus, Mary and Joseph. That's some tongue twister," I laugh in disbelief.

I go to the stand in the shop and pick one to try. They are nice. They taste like our answer to ginger biscuits but only they are thinner and smoother. I buy my parents some tea towels and fridge magnets. I get Rochelle a fridge magnet too. Rochelle and I have a thing, wherever we go in the world we buy each other a fridge magnet. As we walk round the shopping centre some more, I see a gent's shop.

"Mattias, I'm just going to nip in there and get Shane a t-shirt," I say while pointing over to the shop.

"No problem," Mattias says from behind me. I look round but Mattias doesn't seem to be paying attention, he has his eye on a shoe shop and starts walking in the other direction. I nip into the shop and have a look around at the clothes, the one thing I notice with Stockholm is how expensive everything is. I don't know how people can afford to live here – *their wages must be very high*, I think to myself, *as you couldn't possibly afford to live here otherwise*.

I see a nice plain white Levis t-shirt and decide to get Shane that, I check the size then take to the counter and pay. Once I get back out the shop, I find Mattias again, he is still in the shoe shop across the way. He's sitting down taking off his shoes. I walk in to get him.

I've bought all my gifts to take back home and Mattias has got himself a new pair of trainers. We have a glance round a few more shops but feel I'm all shopped out now and my hands are killing me with all the bags.

"I know you work at the hotel, and you probably don't fancy going there especially as you are off on holiday, but do you want to eat there and have a couple of drinks there? I can drop off all these bags if we go."

"Sure, why not. I don't mind. I get a very good staff discount. Let's go," Mattias takes a couple of my bags off me, which I'm quite relieved about if I'm being honest with myself.

We make our way out the shopping mall and start walking down the long street back to The Sheraton. There are a few nice shops outside the shopping mall, but I feel like I've spent a small fortune today and try not to look too long at the windows in case I'm tempted.

Once back at the hotel, I nip up to my room to drop of all my shopping bags then head back down to the bar area in the lobby where Mattias is sitting staring out the window. He appears lost in thought and doesn't notice me walking towards him.

"Boo! You didn't even flinch, Mattias," I say joking.

"It takes more than that to scare me, Chelle," Mattias says laughing.

I sit down across the table from Mattias, where he already has a rose wine on the table waiting for me.

"Thanks for the wine," I say, impressed he's ordered for me already.

"No problem. I thought you would want a rose wine," he says with a smile.

"Good shout. Although when I'm back home, I don't normally drink as much as this. Just for the record," I say laughing but with a seriousness tone also. I feel I have to clarify, as us Irish are known to like a drink or two and I have drunk a lot the last couple of days, but feel this trip has been more like a holiday if I'm being honest. When I go on holiday, I love nothing more than a cheeky wine here and there. Just not when I'm back home.

"Don't worry, I'm not judging you Chelle, you're on vacation. It's what most people do when they are away from their normal reality," he says smiling.

I watch all the hustle and bustle of people walking past, most appear in a hurry, the few that don't appear to be in a hurry appear to be on a leisurely stroll. There are tourists looking at everything and pulling out their camera phones every two minutes.

"When you arrive back in Ireland tomorrow, will you have to go to the office, or can you go straight home?"

"I can go home and just work from home, sending emails, then back into the office on Tuesday as normal. Steve will be fine with me working from home tomorrow."

"I've enjoyed catching up with you after all these years, Chelle. It's been good to see you," Mattias says with a warm smile across his face that stretches to his eyes and highlights the lines that comes to us all with age.

"It's been grand. I can't believe I bumped into you on my first day here. Of all the millions of people that stay in this city, what're the chances?" I say, genuinely shocked.

"I know. It's definitely fate, I think. The stars aligned on Thursday!" he says.

"They sure did. I will keep in touch with you on Facebook and see how you are getting on."

"Yes, definitely and who knows, maybe it won't be another seventeen years until we meet again." Mattias pulls a sad face.

I can't tell if he's joking or if he means it.

"What do you have planned for the rest of your time off, now that you will be getting rid of me?"

"I've enjoyed seeing you. I will probably go see my Mum tomorrow and then catch up with my friends. To be honest, I don't really have any plans set in stone, I'm just enjoying not having to set the alarm clock."

"Sure. I hear ya. I love a Saturday and Sunday no alarm clock. Well, I suppose I technically do have an alarm clock..." Mattias looks at me, puzzled.

"Niamh – my daughter. That wee girl gets me up at the crack of dawn," I say with a smile.

I look out the window: it's just gone teatime and the sun is still high in the sky. I'm quite surprised, I always thought the Scandinavian countries are like Ireland, not that hot and bloody cold, but the weather these past few days has been great.

"Do you get good summers here, Mattias? Only the weather has been great here the past few days and I always thought Sweden would be like Ireland with non-existent summers?"

"No, we generally get good summers in Stockholm. The further north you go in Sweden, the weather gets cooler," he explains while looking out the window.

We decide to go through to the restaurant for dinner, as earlier I said to Mattias because I am up early tomorrow for my flight, I'm not going to have a late night. I want to get to my bed early, so I don't sleep in for my flight. I could imagine me Ma and Shane's reaction if I were to call them and tell them I had missed my flight, not to mention my boss Steve, he would be so pissed with me especially.

We walk into the restaurant which is very big and airy and wait until the waiter comes over to show us to our seats. The waitress acknowledges Mattias, and they chat back and forth. Every so often she looks at me sideways, sizing me up. She's all giggles around him; I think she likes him. I recognise the signs, it's the exact same way I was many years ago. I still like Mattias now, but I can safely say I'm not that way with him. I'm more content and secure in his company now. She takes us to our table by the window and gives us our menus.

"She likes you," I say, leaning over the table and lowering my voice, so she doesn't hear me.

"What? No, she doesn't. I think she's just being nice. It's because I'm her boss," he says, shutting down the conversation quickly.

"I'm a woman and I know when another woman likes a man. I'm telling you, she does," I say persistently, not letting him change the topic too quickly.

"How can you tell?"

"You just can. She reminds me of the way I was with you many years ago. When I would be all giggly. Trust me, she does."

"Are you not that giggly way with me now?" he says, with a menacing smile on his face.

"Your jokes are crap," I say sarcastically.

We both laugh some more then look at the menu.

After dinner, a sad feeling takes over me, as I know I will have to say my goodbyes once more to Mattias and this will probably be the last time we will ever see each other again.

"What's wrong? Mattias asks in as soft, serious tone.

"Och nothing really. I guess I'm sad in a way, this will probably be the last time we will see each other," I say with a half-smile.

Mattias reaches over the table and puts his hand on top of mine then leans over.

"If you get fed up with your fiancé, you know you can always pack a bag and you and Niamh can come and see me."

"You would get a fright if I did," I say laughing.

We both look out the window for a bit, neither of us wanting to be the first to call it a night and say our goodbyes. Our seats are right by the window, and it feels like we have the best views in the place, overlooking the harbour. It's a beautiful night in Stockholm, the sun is reflecting on the water colours of orange and blue. For once there doesn't seem to be that many cars going past the hotel, it feels like everything has stopped in time. Mattias and I make small chit chat about our families and the ever-depressing weather in Ireland that I will be going back to tomorrow.

"If you had the money and could stay anywhere in the world, where would you pick?" he asks, holding my gaze.

"Why?" I ask intrigued, not sure where this conversation is going. "Hmm I've never really thought about it. Maybe the Caribbean."

"Why the Caribbean?" Mattias asks.

"Great weather for one and not pissing rain all the time. Good food and everything slow-paced and a tomorrow-will-do attitude," I say.

"Yes. I suppose. I've never been. The nearest I've got to it is magazines – the beaches look beautiful."

Before he can finish, I interrupt him.

"Why, where would your choice be?"

"Italy. Either Rome or somewhere on the Amalfi coast," he says while looking lost in thought.

"Really. How come?" I ask, being genuinely interested.

"The food and the culture. The history, Italy is steeped in history, and I think the Amalfi coast is beautiful anytime of the year you visit it," he says, turning his stare back towards me.

"I can see why you picked Italy, especially for the food. I've never been but I will put the Amalfi coast on my bucket list now. Even its name sounds very glamorous," I say with a laugh.

Mattias turns to me now with a serious expression on his face.

"I better let you go and get packed and ready for your beauty sleep, or you will miss your flight tomorrow and we can't have that. I've been talking nonstop to you tonight just to get you to stay five minutes longer and putting off the inevitable."

"Are you wanting rid of me, Mattias?" I ask jokingly.

I walk Mattias outside of the hotel and we move slightly away from the front revolving doors not to block them.

"Well, I guess this is goodbye, my old friend," I say sadly, walking towards him to give him a hug.

"I guess it is." He gives me a hug with one arm and his other hand removes the hair from over my eyes.

"I've really enjoyed the past few days with you, Chelle, and I hope you have, too. I wish you well and I will keep in touch now on social media."

"It's been great. Thank you for being such a great host and introducing me to some of your family. I've had a lovely time," I say sincerely.

We give each other another embrace and with that, Mattias gives me a kiss on the forehead. We then say our goodbyes and I turn back to the hotel, not daring to look around again.

Chapter Twenty-Seven

As the plane touches back down in Dublin, already Stockholm is starting to feel like a dream. I enjoyed my few days away and yes; I did meet up with an ex, but I tell myself nothing happened. I will just leave out the Mattias part of Stockholm when I tell Niamh and Shane how my trip went. Although it keeps playing with my conscious lying to them but, I keep trying to remind myself I'm not lying, I'm just missing a bit out, there's a difference. Changing the subject in my head to take my mind off it, I now start running through a list of things I need to do now I'm back.

As everyone vacates the plane, we are all like penguins in a line leaving one by one. *I hate this bit*, I think to myself, *I'm so glad I don't fly as often now.* I head on down to the carousel to pick up my luggage and I'm in luck, I'm not waiting for long before I see my case. I pick it up, then make my way to the exit, where I can hopefully get a taxi. As I walk through the arrivals, I see Shane giving me a wave. *What's he doing here?* I think to myself. *He's never here to pick me up.*

"What are you doing here, shouldn't you be at work?"

"Work's quiet and it's not even eleven yet. I thought I would surprise you," he says with a smile.

"Oh, thanks, that was nice of you," I say giving him a hug.

Shane takes my case, and we proceed to walk to the exit to where he has parked his car.

"Where's me Ma, is she back at ours? Or is she away into Dublin shopping?" I ask, looking forward to showing her all the souvenirs I got her and my Da.

A worried look comes over Shane's face with an expression I can't read, but his whole-body language now is making me nervous.

"What's wrong with me Ma, Shane?" I scream.

"Nothing, your Ma's fine. She went away back home yesterday," he says, looking down at the ground, unable to give me eye contact now.

"What, why? She was supposed to be staying with us to help with Niamh until I got back. What's going on?" I ask, feeling the annoyance starting to rise from within. My patience is getting shorter.

"Your ma is fine. There is a couple of things I need to tell you. Can it please wait until we get to the car, and we have privacy," he says finally, lifting his eyes to meet mine.

I start to feel sick and worry what has been going on. Why did my mother take off back home, she normally loves coming to see us. *I know they argued the other day, is it something to do with that?* I wonder to myself. The long walk back to the car feels like an eternity. I can feel my stomach churning with what is Shane going to tell me. Has my Ma and Shane had another argument?

Shane opens the boot of his car and puts my case in. I get into the passenger seat and see a big bottle of water hardly touched. I start to feel like I have a dry mouth, and I pick up the water and take a large drink of it as Shane gets into the car.

I turn to him before he's even started up the car or has his seat belt on.

"Right Shane tell me, what's going on?" I demand.

"Let me drive away first," he says, staring at his car keys.

"No, tell me now," I shout.

"Okay, okay. On Friday night I got a bit drunk at the golf club and then a few of us went back to Peter's for more drinks and before I knew it, I fell asleep at Peter's and didn't wake up 'till the morning. As soon as I woke up, I went straight home, and yer Ma was up, and she wasn't impressed with me walking in at eight am in the morning. She started shouting and accusing me of all sorts. With all the shouting, Niamh woke up and came down the stairs and we stopped arguing," he says now, staring out the window, unable to look at me.

"Accusing you of what?" I ask, probing but having a fair idea what he's talking about. I just need him to say it out loud.

"She thought I had another woman or something and she left yesterday saying, 'If you don't tell Michelle then I will.'" Shane now turns to look at me.

All I can think about is my poor daughter in the middle of me Ma and Shane's argument and witnessing all this.

"Did Niamh hear all this?" I ask, starting to feel sick.

"No. Yer Ma calmed down when Niamh came down and she said it to me quietly yesterday she was leaving and that I better tell you. Niamh doesn't know anything is wrong," he says in a quiet tone.

Thank God, I think to myself.

"That's not like me Ma. There must have been more to it, for me Ma to go mad like that. Me Ma isn't that kind of person," I say now feeling the anger rise inside of me.

I watch Shane's face change and he appears to swallow hard; his expression isn't one I've seen before from him and I'm unable to read it, but if I was to guess he looks scared, almost as though he's going to cry. He appears to say something, but nothing comes out. Just then I remembered something and reach into my passenger side of the car. I flick through the bits of paper and I see it there in front of me. I knew at the time deep down what it was, but for Niamh's sake, chose to ignore it.

"What's this, Shane?" I ask.

"What's what?" he says looking at the bit of paper I'm holding up.

He snatches it out of my hand and as soon as he sees what is written on the receipt, he swallows hard again.

"Well, who did you take there? Because it certainly wasn't me. You've never said you had to go to Donegal for work," I say angrily, trying to keep my voice from getting higher.

"Eh, eh. Listen, Michelle, this isn't how it looks," he says talking fast now.

I can feel myself getting mad. I reach over to the driver's side and pull the keys out of the car.

"We are not going anywhere until you tell me the truth. We can stay here all day until I start getting answers," I scream. I see a woman turn around as she walks past the car, but I don't care. I'm unable to take my tone down a notch. I'm angrier now than anything else.

Shane takes a long deep breath and puts his head on the steering wheel. He turns to face me and he looks as though his world has collapsed with sad eyes. Suddenly I feel my breathing getting faster and I can feel myself coming out in a cold sweat, there's not enough air in this car for the two of us. I feel like I can't breathe. I reach to the left of me to put the window down in the car so I can get air and turn back to look at him.

"I love you and Niamh, you're both my world, I'm really sorry, I've been such a fool," he says, quietly trying to reach over to grab my hand. I quickly pull away.

"Go on," I say with no real emotion in my voice; I need to hear what's coming next.

"A few months back, you and I weren't getting on and this girl at the Golf Club started showing me a bit of attention. It started off with harmless flirting."

Before he can carry on his story, I butt in: "What's her name?"

"Kayleigh," he says, staring down.

"Kayleigh, what? Do I know her?" I ask.

"No. Her second name is Coffey. She was there with her friends when I first bumped into her," he says while looking back out the window, unable to look at me.

As Shane keeps talking, I can feel my stomach going from feeling sick like I really need to throw up to anger, pure rage.

"Sorry, say that again," I snap.

"Well, one thing led to another over time and then before I knew it, we were having an affair. You're right, I took her to that hotel. The guilt was killing me," he says, looking down at his legs.

"The guilt was killing you that it went on for a few months, Shane. Really?" I say sarcastically.

"Please let me finish. I tried breaking it off a few times and she threatened to tell you. I was scared, I didn't want to lose you or Niamh," Shane says slowing his words now.

"No. You wanted to have your cake and eat it, didn't you," I say very matter of fact.

"It's not like that, Michelle," he says in a pleading voice.

"Tell me one thing, how did my mother put two and two together that this was going on and I've been living under the same roof as you for months and hadn't a clue. Did she come to her house? Did my mum walk in on you both?" I say, feeling like I'm going to start crying.

"I made up my mind, that I was going to break it off. I had

been trying to for ages. Then on Friday she was really upset when I told her it was over, so I stayed with her and ended up falling asleep at hers. When I woke up, it was six am and I headed straight home and told her never to contact me again, we were over," Shane said, looking me straight in the eyes.

"You mean you had one last rendezvous with her before you called it off." Again, I give him a sarcastic answer back.

He doesn't say anything, he just leans back in his chair and looks dead ahead.

"I know you hate me just now, Michelle, but I feel so much better for telling you. It's like a big weight has been lifted off my shoulders. We can honestly work through this," he says, grabbing my hand.

"Don't touch me. I don't want you near me. Let go of my hand. Do you feel better now that you've said your penance? Well, if you think I'm going to be Father Campbell and absolve you of your sins by three hail Mary's you have another thing coming," I say, mocking him.

Still, Shane persists. "I know you're angry and I'm going to give you time, but we can work through this. I know how stupid I've been. I'm truly sorry for hurting you."

I start joining the dots and it's all starting to make sense now. Like a light bulb coming on in my head.

"A few weeks ago, I was talking to Mark the accountant at work, and he said he knew you but looking back he changed the subject straight away. I must be the talk of work. 'Poor Michelle.'" I start to cry, feeling like such a fool.

"Aye, erm I got talking to Mark one night when she was there, and I was a bit drunk and he said where he worked..." He trails off.

I stop listening to Shane halfway through the conversation and join the rest of the dots up myself. Mark is on my Facebook and if Shane had been drunk, he's probably let it slip or something and Mark has realised who Shane is when I've posted pictures of us. I can't blame Mark, he's probably felt so awkward as soon as he said he knew Shane and then made a run for it when he said he had to get back to work. On the Saturday when I was in Sweden, he was texting me because he had broken it off with his floozy and been caught by my mother. *Jesus, I feel like such a fool*, I think to myself. Now the tears come fast, tearing down my face and cheeks.

"You were only texting me all that lovey dovey shit because you were caught and feeling sorry for yourself. You knew what was coming when my Ma gave you the ultimatum to tell me. Instead of thinking about me, you were thinking about yourself, about poor Shane," I say, struggling to get the rest of my words out through the tears and temper.

Shane sits quietly not saying a word. With my jacket sleeve, I wipe the tears and snot from my face. I sit staring dead ahead, trying to compose myself.

"I want you gone, out the house for a few days. I need to think, and I can't bear to be around you just now. Please, just take me home," I say, holding my head. I feel such a headache coming on.

Shane lets out a deep breath and starts the car engine. I have so many questions going round my head, I'm thinking that much I feel my head's going to explode. I reach over and take another sip from the water bottle. I turn away from Shane and stare out my window, I don't really focus on anything, just my own thoughts. I could pass anything, or anyone right now and not notice. I have more questions for him but right now I feel mentally exhausted and this was not the welcome home I had expected to receive. We drive the whole way back without saying a word to each other; I can barely look at him but every so often I catch him out of the corner of my eye looking over at me. As we pull into the drive, I turn to him.

"Take your stuff and leave, I need to be alone," I say firmly.

"Okay," Shane says quietly.

I feel angry now, I feel my whole body burning now with rage. As I close the car door behind me, I don't realise the force I use until I hear the banging of the door behind me. Shane is already trying to get my suitcase out the back of his car, I reach over to the handle and pull it off him before taking the case myself and marching into the house. I leave my case sitting in the hall before throwing myself on the couch and lying back as my head feels as though it's going to explode, it's pounding now. I hear the floorboards from upstairs creak as Shane walks about, packing his stuff. When he is finished, he comes back downstairs.

"I'm honestly very sorry Michelle, I truly am. Do you want me to pick Niamh up from school?" Shane asks.

"No, you're fine. I will get her myself. I've not saw her for a few days, so I will pick her up," I say flatly.

"Okay, I will call you in a few days," Shane says while closing the door behind him.

I don't turn around and don't respond to his last comment. I just lie on the couch with my own thoughts and a heavy heart. I decide to close my eyes as it might stop my head from hurting and give my mind some peace. I set an alarm clock on my phone an hour before Niamh gets out of school so I can get myself organised before I pick her up. I lie back on the couch and curl myself up into the fetal position and lie on my side to face the TV. I close my eyes and can feel myself just about to nod off when I hear my phone ringing. I check who it is that's calling before I answer the call.

"Hi Ma," I say.

"So, you've spoken to Shane, then," she says calmly and softly.

"How did you know, Ma?" I ask.

"I could see it all over his face and he reeked of perfume when he came in the door, I just knew. I told him you better tell Chelle, or I will, but he kept denying it," she explains letting out a sigh.

"Ma, my head is bursting, can I call you later once I get Niamh to bed," I feel totally wiped out now talking to her and I just want to lie down and close my eyes trying not to think or speak anyone.

I hang up the phone and then put it on silent. I want to switch off from people for a bit to overcome this headache and to gather my own thoughts. I feel mentally exhausted and it's not even midday yet. I close my eyes once more.

Chapter Twenty-Eight

After dozing off for two hours, I awake to my alarm going off and feel a bit groggy. My head doesn't feel as heavy and sore, but I still have the sickness feeling in my stomach. I lie still for a few minutes after switching off my alarm and think how it came to this, how did this happen to me. How did my Ma know before me, was I really that stupid, I couldn't see what was going on in front of me. All the weekends at the golf club, Mark from my work knowing about it and not me. As I'm thinking about Mark from my work, I make a mental note in my head that I will need to call Steve and say I've come down with something: work is the last place I want to be right now.

Thinking about it all once more, if I'm really honest with myself, I think I've always known. I've just not wanted to confront it or really think about it too much for Niamh's sake. To rock her wee world upside down. All the trips to the golf club I did know, I just didn't want to admit it to myself. Never underestimate a person's sixth sense.

I pull myself up from the couch and go through to the

kitchen to get a glass of water, I catch my reflection in the mirror on my way through to the kitchen. I stand and look at myself for a few minutes. My eyes look heavy, the glow I had the other day is gone, I see a few lines forming in my forehead and around my eyes. *Get a grip*, I think to myself, *now is not the time to be observing my appearance.* I've just got up at a god-awful time and caught a flight only to be told terrible news in a car park, my partner's been having an affair, of course I'm not going to be looking like Cindy Crawford. As quickly as it comes into my head, it leaves my thoughts again, I've got bigger things to worry about than a few bloody wrinkles.

I grab a glass of water then tie my hair back and grab my car keys and head on out the door to get Niamh from school. As I drive over to the school, the traffic is good today and I get to the school gates early. I park up and see a few of the other parents standing waiting for their children. I recognise a couple of them, but I really don't want to make small talk with anyone today. I sit in the car and wait until I hear the bell ringing. Once it rings, I get out the car and walk up the short path. As I'm walking up to get Niamh, I pull out my phone and decide to see what she looks like on Facebook. I type her name in Kayleigh Coffey, but nothing comes up in the search. I put it in a couple of times and change the spelling slightly of the second name but again nothing comes up. I start dialling Rochelle's number and think I will tell her what's been going on, but it just rings out onto voicemail. I hang up and don't leave a voicemail as she will see my number, and I know she will call me back.

As I get to the top of the playground, all the kids are coming out from the school doors. Now is a good time to arrive as all the other parents are too busy looking for their child that they don't notice me. Only once they have their child and they turn to walk away do I get the odd hello from some I know. I look through the crowd of children now in the playground all looking for their parents and I see Niamh, so I give her a wave.

"Mummy!" Niamh shouts, running towards me.

I kneel to give her a cuddle. I'm not sure who's going to benefit more from the cuddle today, Niamh or me.

"Hello chicken. I've missed you; I got you a nice present from Sweden," I say as I pull her in close to me to give her the biggest hug.

"What is it?" she asks with excitement in her voice.

"You'll see when we get back home," I say, smiling.

I take her by the hand and throw her school bag over my right shoulder. As we walk to the car, I ask her how her days been and what she was doing at school all day. I'm careful not to show her how sad I feel inside and constantly keep a smile on my face. So much so that my facial muscles are beginning to feel a bit sore.

When we get back home, Niamh wants to see her surprise from Sweden. My case is still in the living room where I left it earlier. I open it up and rummage through the case to find her presents I bought her. I hand it over to her and as she looks in the bag, her wee face lights up with delight.

"Thanks Mammy," she says grinning from ear to ear, not taking her eyes off her new toys.

I start unpacking the rest of my case and take my dirty washing and place it in the washing machine. I realise I never checked to see if there was anything in for dinner tonight. Food is the last thing on my mind just now, but I need to make something for Niamh's dinner. I check the freezer and there is a Margherita pizza. *I will just throw that in the oven and she can have that tonight*, I think to myself. I'm not going to win mother of the year award tonight cooking, but I'm not bothered she usually gets a good, varied diet and tonight is a one off and won't hurt her.

As I come back through to the living room, Niamh is playing with her new doll and her teddy. That will keep her entertained for a while. I really don't have the energy to do anything, but I must keep pushing myself on for Niamh's sake, as I don't want her to know there is anything wrong.

"Listen Niamh. Daddy had to go and work away for a few days, so it's just me and you. Do you want to sleep in my bed tonight?"

"Okay," Niamh says not lifting her eyes once. She's too busy playing with her new toys.

I leave Niamh playing in the living room and when I take my case back upstairs to put it away, I try calling Rochelle once more. She still doesn't answer. I leave her a voicemail this time telling her to call me it's important but to call after eight pm, when Niamh is in bed.

The night quickly passes from making Niamh dinner to helping her with her homework and laying out her school clothes for tomorrow and then getting her bathed and ready for bed.

"Okay Mrs. You can sleep in my bed tonight. It's a quick story then off to bed," I say in a serious tone.

Niamh gives a big grin the minute I mention she is sleeping in my bed tonight.

"Pick a story, which one are you thinking?" Niamh studies her bookshelf for a few moments and then decides.

"This one," she pulls down Elsa and Anna.

She runs past me, through to my room and jumps straight up on the bed. I already closed the blinds and the curtains earlier when she was in the bath. Like all parents I have routine for bedtime and try not to waver from it. I sit up on my bed beside her and start reading to her. The more I turn the pages, the more Niamh's eyes seem to be getting heavier.

"Right chicken, that's enough for tonight. Come on, it's time for bed," I say giving her a gentle kiss on the forehead.

"Night, night Mammy," she says quietly.

"Night. I will be up shortly, as Mammy is tired too. Love you," I reach over and give her another kiss once more.

"Love you too, Mammy," she quickly rolls over onto her side and lets out a yawn.

I pull the covers up and tuck her in and leave the room closing the door but leaving it open ever so slightly.

When I get back downstairs, I start washing the couple of dishes that are in the sink, only to hear my mobile ringing in the living room. Oh, Christ that will wake Niamh up. I run through to answer it quickly before it rings anymore.

"What's wrong?" Rochelle asks in a worried voice before I can say hello.

I proceed to start telling Rochelle everything that has happened since arriving back in Ireland today. I start to jump back and forth about receipts, and Mark from my work.

"Right, calm down and take it back to the very start," Rochelle says firmly.

As I go back to the start and tell Rochelle everything, I start to feel sick and sad again. When I was getting Niamh organised, my mind was preoccupied and now I'm back with these horrible feels swirling around inside me.

"What a bastard," Rochelle says in very Rochelle style not holding anything back, saying exactly what she means.

"I can't believe it took for me Ma to be here for all this to come out," I say, sighing.

"Maybe, deep down you did know, but you just didn't want to admit it to yourself," Rochelle says in a soft, sympathetic tone.

Rochelle's words linger in my head a while that I don't listen to the rest of what she's saying to me. I don't have the heart to tell Rochelle that she's right. I had a fair idea but buried my head in the sand, not wanting to rock Niamh's world. So I behaved like a door mat. Now, I feel angry and ashamed of myself for not confronting things before it got to this point. I start to feel sick and loathe myself. Is that why I went gallivanting all over Sweden with my ex, to secretly piss off Shane? I don't know, I have so many thoughts going through my head just now that I'm starting to get a sore head again. I wish I was a psychologist, then I would know why I behave the way I behave.

"Rochelle, I need to go. I'm done in and want to get an early night, I will call you tomorrow. Thanks for listening and don't say anything to anyone, will you not please. As I want to keep this to myself a while longer before I decide what I'm going to do for the best," I say flatly.

"No, don't worry I won't say a thing, that's your business, but you know I'm here any time for you. Pack your bags and run off to Sweden, that will bloody teach him," she says with a laugh in true Rochelle style. She is trying to get me to laugh, but I just can't see the funny side and let out a sigh. Normally I would laugh but not today.

I come off the phone to Rochelle and choose not to do anymore cleaning or tidying up and just get myself off to bed. I've had a horrible day my head is thumping once more. I pour myself a glass of water and go around switching off all the lights downstairs.

Chapter Twenty-Nine

A couple of weeks have passed since that awful day. I'm making small steps with Shane; today I'm meeting him in town for lunch. I have started letting him stay over in the spare room, just for Niamh's sake. Every other day he's telling me how sorry he is and that nothing like that will ever happen again if I give him one more chance. I have moments where I feel I can put it all behind me and take baby steps to trust him again, which will then swing to anger that it wasn't just a one night stand: it was a full-blown affair and how can I ever trust him again?

As I make my way to the cafe which is around the corner from my work, I catch a glimpse of my reflection in one of the long office windows I pass. I've lost a bit of weight, probably with all the stress I've been under recently. Like any woman, it's given me a newfound confidence shifting that extra seven pounds, even if it was under the most terrible circumstances; seven pounds is seven pounds less.

As I walk into the cafe, I see it is quite busy, most people are dressed in suits, and I presume their offices aren't far away and like me they have just ran out to get a bite to eat. I look to the back of the cafe and see Shane sitting there already patiently waiting on me. He sees me as I walk in and gets up to greet me. He goes to give me a hug and reluctantly I give him one back. I still feel a bit strange giving him a hug, maybe this this too will pass with time.

"You look great. I love your hair," he says while touching my hair.

"Thanks," I say coyly.

Yesterday I went to the hairdressers and decided I wanted something different; I went for a long bob. My hair was down my back before, but I wanted something radical and then proceeded to get a long bob and go lighter with very blonde highlights. I always dyed my brown hair a lighter tone of brown and thought after years of keeping it the same hairstyle it was time for a new me to new beginnings starting with the hair.

"I've ordered, Michelle, what are you fancying?" Shane asks while I'm studying the menu.

"I think I'm going to go for a tomato and basil soup with bread and butter. I don't fancy a lot, just something light," I say while still checking out the menu.

The waiter comes by and asks if I'm ready to give my order. Once I order, I turn to Shane to give him my full attention as I feel I need to try.

"So, how was your day?" I ask.

"It was alright. You know we are quite quiet just now. What about yours?" he asks and appears to be genuinely interested.

"Yeah it was alright. We've been quite busy with a few new orders. Sinead is coming back next week, so hopefully that will take some of the pressure off me," I say with a feeling of relief.

"Is she?" Shane says still looking interested.

"Yeah, why?" I ask wondering why he's interested in Sinead; he's never met her.

"Well, I was going to ask if you and Niamh would like to go on holiday in the next couple of weeks with me, I could organise something. We could go abroad or stay in Ireland, just time away for the three of us. I think it would be good for us all," he says smiling.

I stare at Shane, while thinking to myself. Yes, it would be good for Niamh to have a holiday and he is trying to make amends; should I go on the holiday and see what it's like just the three of us for a week and then make my mind up once and for all if we are going to be able to salvage this relationship? I now feel if I'm going to try and make a go of it with Shane then I need to tell him about Sweden and my old friend because if I don't then I'm just as bad as Shane. Although technically nothing happened, it was two people meeting; but still, I had history with this man once and I'm a firm believer in if something must stay a secret then it should never have taken off in the first place.

"Sure, why not. It would be good for Niamh to get a holiday. There is just something I need to speak to you about," I say in a nervous tone.

"What's wrong?" Shane says reaching over the table to put his hand on top of mine, looking at me.

"I don't want to do this here. I would rather speak about it tonight," I say, looking around at how busy the cafe is getting and not wanting our dirty washing aired in public.

I see the waiter coming out with two soup bowls and I'm hoping they are ours. Saved in the nick of time. The lovely aroma of basil hits me just as the waiter puts the dishes down at our table. As I put the spoon to my mouth, I can feel the heat and quickly put the soup spoon back down, careful not to burn myself. I then stir my spoon round the bowl for a bit.

"Do you not like it?" Shane asks observing that I appear to be playing with my food.

"No, it's not that. I nearly burnt myself, it was roasting so I'm just trying to cool it down," I say looking up at Shane.

"I was thinking this weekend. I could ask my parents if they would watch Niamh, then you and I could have some time to ourselves. Go out for dinner or something, what do you think?" Shane asks, looking intently at me.

"Yeah maybe, we'll see Shane. I just want to take it one day at a time."

As soon as I've said the words out loud, I start to feel bad internally, as I know he is trying. I change the subject quickly.

Later after we have eaten all our lunch, I check my watch and my hour lunch break is nearly up.

"I better get back to work. It's the quickest hour of the day," I say with a sigh.

We pay our bill and step back out into the back streets of Dublin. Shane walks me the short distance back to my work. Then he turns to me and I feel that he may try and kiss me, but he looks a bit awkward. I take a step back, keeping a slight distance between us. I start to feel a bit uncomfortable with the current situation and don't want to make matters worse. I simply give him a smile and tell him I will see him tonight and to enjoy the rest of his day.

As I stand putting the dishes away, I'm on edge waiting for Shane to walk through the door at any minute. I'm nervous, but once I get this off my chest I will feel better. Especially if we are going to give it another go, I want to be completely honest. Shane phoned earlier to say he will take Niamh after school over to his mum's so that we can have a chat away from her. I feel sick to the pit of my stomach but can't back out. I must get this out as I've been feeling bad about the whole thing since I came back from Sweden. I feel really guilty and can't live with myself. When I first came back and found out everything that Shane did, I didn't feel bad. I felt it was his karma and he deserved it, but now I feel awful that I've not said anything, and I will just be glad once everything is out in the open and we can put it all behind us.

My doorbell rings and it makes me jump back to the present away from my thoughts. *Who is it?* I wonder, *I'm not expecting anyone.* Probably the Jehovah's Witnesses they have been doing the rounds lately, they've a terrible habit of coming to the door when you least expect it. I will tell them I'm just heading out. The doorbell goes again – jeezo, will they give me a minute.

As I open the door, the shape looks like a familiar person but it can't be, I say aloud.

"Hello Chelle. I needed to see you in person. To tell you again, you're making a big mistake," Mattias says, edging his way into my home.

I'm speechless, at a loss for words. I let Mattias walk right past me into my home, forgetting and oblivious to the fact that Shane will be here any minute. I told Mattias everything that happened and what I had found out that day I arrived back from Stockholm. A couple of weeks ago when Shane was still out of the house, I had a couple of wines and told him on messenger, he then called me, and we were on the phone for ages. We've been messaging back and forth every day since. Yesterday, I said to Mattias that I was going to tell Shane about Sweden, for Niamh's sake, that I didn't want any more secrets. I was going to give it another go with Shane and, that if I was honest with myself, deep down, I knew there was something not right for a long time between us, but I smoothed over it for

Niamh. I didn't want her growing up in a broken home and half suspected there was another woman. I'm ashamed to say that I guess that's why part of me liked bumping into an old boyfriend, to take my mind off my reality. I explained all this to Mattias yesterday; I just didn't think he would then jump on a plane to Dublin.

"What are you doing here, Mattias, how do you know where I live?" are the only words I can find right now, still dumbfounded about the whole situation.

"I messaged Rochelle and told her I was in Dublin and needed to see you and asked her for your address," he says quietly.

Going by my face, I think Mattias can guess I am more than upset. I can feel the temper rising from within. I can't believe Rochelle would do that and not mention a word to me.

Just then I hear the door opening. Oh sweet Jesus this is all we need now. I've gone from being nervous to angry back to feeling anxious now that Shane is home.

"Hi Michelle," Shane says trailing off when his eyes catch our visitor.

"Hi Shane. Sorry, this is my friend Mattias. He's just leaving," I say looking towards Mattias.

There is now suddenly an atmosphere in our home. If I can feel it, I'm guessing they both can feel it too. The walls feel like they are getting closer and closer, I feel sick to the pit of my stomach and the enormity of what I've done has now hit me. I look to Mattias once more giving him the eyes, hoping that he will leave.

"Right, yes, I better be going. I will call you later, Chelle," Mattias says nodding while walking to the door.

I mouth a thank you to Mattias, even although I am still a bit annoyed with him for thinking it was okay to jump on a plane and come look me up. I turn to face Shane; I can tell by his face he's heard an accent coming from Mattias and is wondering who he is.

"What's going on? Who's he, *Chelle*?" Shane asks sarcastically at Mattias calling me Chelle. Shane has never called me that, only ever Michelle. Although at times I'm sure he's had a few choice names for me, but definitely not Chelle.

"Sit down. This is what I wanted to speak to you about," I say with a sigh. I can now feel my stomach doing somersaults.

I start to explain to Shane who Mattias is and that I accidentally bumped into him in Sweden. At first, Shane doesn't believe me that nothing happened and that we just so happened to run into each other after all these years.

"Look, I get you're annoyed. I would be too, but I didn't do anything with him. It wasn't me that had the affair for God knows how many months. It was more like bumping into an old friend I haven't seen for years," I say, snapping at Shane.

I can feel myself getting a bit angry now that he is turning this round and is trying to be the victim. It's all about him, he's forgetting he's been having a full-on relationship with someone for months behind my back. I never did anything of the sort with Mattias.

"Well, Michelle. What am I supposed to think when an ex turns up at our house and flies halfway around the world to see if you're okay? What would you think? He clearly still has feelings for you. People don't just jump on planes and go look up their ex when they are having a hard time. That's nuts. Don't act the goat," Shane says angrily.

"I don't know why he's jumped on a plane; I will call him. I've not given him the impression that anything was going to happen between us or lead him on, that I can promise you," I say in a serious tone.

"I wasn't expecting all this tonight when you wanted a chat. I'm going to go and stay with my parents tonight and take some time to get this all straight in my head. It seems I'm not the only one with secrets Michelle, am I?" Shane says with a sneering tone. He then gets up and walks to the door.

I fall back on to the couch, exhausted with the turn of events and think for a minute and try and catch my breath. I don't bother pleading with Shane or asking him to stay; it's probably best for us all that we all get some head space. My thoughts then turn to Rochelle. I can't believe Rochelle would give Mattias my address, and why would Mattias fly all that way just to see me. Have I encouraged him, have I given him the wrong impression? This is all my fault, just when Shane and I were going to try and make a go of it.

I call Mattias and he answers on the third ring.

"Mattias, you shouldn't have come over here. Why did you come, have I led you on?" I say, trying to keep my voice measured.

After a short pause, Mattias answers.

"Yes, I guess it was stupid. No, you didn't lead me on. I felt sorry for you when you told me what happened with Shane, and I enjoyed your company so much in Sweden. I just wanted to see you again," Mattias says quietly.

My thoughts are now racing away in front of me. Mattias feels sorry for me, I don't want his sympathy. I don't know what I was expecting Mattias to tell me, but it wasn't that. I must get off this phone. I'm now feeling stupid and angry that Mattias pities me.

"I don't need your empathy, Mattias. I'm a big girl, I need to go now. Thanks for being a shoulder to cry on but you can get back on the plane to Sweden. I don't need any man, not you and certainly not Shane. Goodbye Mattias," I say putting down the phone.

No sooner have I put the phone down, I feel bad that I've taken my anger out on Mattias.

I pick up my phone once more and start calling Rochelle.

"Chelle, I'm sorry. I know you will probably be mad with me. I thought I was doing the right thing," Rochelle says with no more than a whisper.

I don't interrupt her. I listen to what she has to say, more because I don't have the energy to argue with anyone. Rochelle tells me that Mattias messaged her and that he was worried about me, and she thought in her grand wisdom that him coming over here would give Shane a fright and it would do my self-esteem some good. She says that she only had the best intentions for me, she said that Mattias is here for three days and is staying at the Premier Inn in the centre of Dublin on Gloucester Street. I then tell her what went down earlier and how I feel exhausted with everything.

"I forgive you, Rochelle, just please don't do anything like that again. Hopefully there isn't going to be a next time, but if there is please run something like that past me first," I say letting out a sigh.

"I promise I won't act the goat again. I will absolutely tell you if I ever get a brain wave like this again. I'm sorry Chelle, but you've got to admit. It is a bit comical that he's actually got on that plane and flown over here. It says a lot about him and what he thinks of you," she says with a bit of humour in her voice.

I let out a heavy sigh once more and do agree with her on that. It was nice of him, or crazy of him – I'm not sure which word I would use to describe him jumping on the plane to come over and see me. Regret starts flooding through me when I remember the look on his face when I asked him to go. I feel the remorse is going to kill me and conclude I better go and see him and not leave it like this before it's too late.

I pick up my car keys and run out the door. No sooner have I got in the car than I am at the hotel. The drive over was a blur,

I couldn't tell if there was traffic or if I was playing music in the car, I was so engrossed in my own thoughts and fixated on getting here and making right the wrong I said. As I walk into the hotel, the reception is straight ahead, there is no one at the desk. I look around to the left, where the bar and restaurant is and there sitting by the window, I see a lone familiar face.

Epilogue

2 Years later – 2017

I catch a glimpse of myself in the mirror and it's hard not to notice my expanding tummy. I never imagined myself walking down the aisle at five months pregnant. Rochelle watches me admiring myself in the mirror while patting my tummy.

"You look grand. You're very neat. You should have saw me at five months, I was twice your size," she says with a warm smile that lights up her face.

"I just didn't imagine that I would be waddling down the aisle," I say laughing.

Niamh comes bounding through looking beautiful in her flower girl dress. It's white with a light pink ribbon all the way around and ties at the back, with three pink flowers at the front. At the bottom of the dress, there are some pink petals caught by white mesh, unable to fall out. Her hair is all ringlets falling down to her shoulders with a hairband keeping everything perfectly in place.

"Oh, Niamh, you look lovely," I say admiring her as she twirls around in her dress.

"So do you, Mammy," she says reaching in to give me a cuddle.

I look at the two of us now in the mirror. My dress is cream: it's tight fitting around the bust area, and just under the bust it's loose and floaty. The top of my dress is heavily patterned with short sleeves and a slight plunging bust line. The top part of my dress has pearls and crystals through it, while the bottom part is very plain and covers my ever-expanding bump nicely. I have my hair half up and half down with a long veil which has a flower pattern at the sides all the way down and around. I have chosen to keep my makeup very natural with a light pink lipstick.

My Ma and Da come through to my hotel room. My Da is holding three glasses and my Ma is carrying champagne.

"Sorry lass, none for you," he says while setting up the three glasses.

"I know," I say patting my stomach.

My Da hands round the glasses to my Ma and Rochelle.

Rochelle takes the glass off My Da. "Don't worry, Chelle, we will have plenty for ya.

"You sure you want to go through with this, there's still time for you to be the runaway bride," me Ma says with a poker face then bursts out laughing.

The look on my face must say it all. "I'm only kidding with you, love," she says and puts her hand out to grab mine reassuringly.

The four of us sit about, talking and laughing while Niamh plays with her dolls. I feel a bit nervous inside, I walk to the balcony of my hotel room which is overlooking the garden grounds of the hotel we are staying at. It's beautiful – all the greenery and exotic lush flowers with the swimming pool in the middle then just a little further you can see the white sand and sea. The water is so clear and beautiful even from up here you can still hear the rolling crashing of the waves. As I stand for a bit, I can already feel myself starting to melt and it's just gone four pm here. Although my dress is long, I was careful not to pick something to heavy as I knew I would be sweltering in this exotic climate, so far removed from Ireland and to what I'm used to.

"Chelle, that's just gone four we better start making our way down," my Da shouts through from the other room.

I step back inside and within seconds I already feel cooler with the air con on and blasting. I go and pour myself a large water. My Ma heads downstairs to take her seat, beside my brother and sister and their families, it's just the four of us left. I hand Niamh her flower girl basket with rose petals in it and then take Rochelle's bouquet out the box and it to her, then grab mine, admiring the beautiful cream rose display.

"Now remember, Niamh, tell me what you've to do again with the rose petals," I ask bending down to my daughter.

"When we walk down the aisle mammy, I have to throw them out," she says twirling round.

I take her hand and we all walk out of the room. Rochelle ensures everything except the air-con is turned off, locks up then follows behind us. As we get downstairs to the hotel lobby, Sonny our wedding planner is waiting for us.

"You look lovely my darling. Give me a twirl," he says with a genuine smile.

He probably does this about five days a week, but you could never tell he seems excited all the same as though it's his first wedding he's ever done, and I have to say these past seven days he has been great. Nothing is too much trouble or a bother for him and he makes you feel at ease.

"Right this way, guys," Sonny instructs.

He takes us through a side way of the open-air restaurant and over the bridge at the swimming pool then along down to the path at the beach. I can just make out the start of the altar and rows of chairs laid out and down the middle a red carpet leading to the makeshift altar which is slightly under a tree. I picked that spot to give a bit a shade from the beating sun. Even as the sun starts to set in Barbados, it's still warm and humid, due to where it lies near the equator. Plus, I thought the spot was nice and intimate.

As soon as the organist sees me from the distance, he starts playing Here Comes the Bride but with a Caribbean twist to it. Rochelle and Niamh walk on in front of me and true to her word the wee soul drops the rose petals one by one. I have my Da's arm as he walks me up the altar.

The closer I get to the top of the aisle, the more I can see that familiar smile beaming away at me and keeping his eyes firmly on me. The sun is shining down on him and our minister. As I pass some of my family and close friends and some of his family, I smile all the same. I feel so happy inside, nothing could take the smile off my face. Once I get to the top of the aisle, me Da gives me a kiss then turns to shake Mattias' hand and turns back around to go and take his seat beside my mum, brother, and sister.

"You look beautiful," Mattias whispers into my ear.

"You scrub up not bad yourself," I say jokingly.

We both then turn to face the minister.

I think to myself as the minster starts to speak. About the last two years and how we got here. I tried to make it work with Shane for Niamh's sake, but, ultimately, I couldn't forgive him for what he had done. It may have been different if it were just a one-night stand, I would have been hurt all the same, but the fact that it went on for several months and in the end, everyone knew except me, I just couldn't do it. I felt a fool and I couldn't look at him in that way anymore; I had changed and so had he. He still sees Niamh all the time and I encourage that relationship; I have never been one of those people that would stop him from seeing his child. Even when he was having the affair his fathering skills and love of Niamh never altered. He is a great dad to Niamh, and the only person it would hurt would be Niamh.

Mattias and I spoke daily over messenger. I took it slow to start with and then, about a year in, I introduced him to Niamh, and they get on well. She will run up to him whenever she sees him and gives him a cuddle and that's half the battle; she's happy and I'm happy.

Mattias has recently moved over to Dublin to live with me. I have a small apartment which is a bit further out of Dublin and not so close to Niamh's school but it's fine, it will do for now. Shane and I are civil to each other, we always put Niamh's wellbeing first. He's on to his third girlfriend since we split up. Thankfully, he doesn't introduce them all to Niamh and, to be honest, I really don't care. I wish him well.

I knew when I jumped in the car that night and drove over to see Mattias at the hotel that my mind was made up. We sat chatting for ages that night, and the next morning I called Shane and told him I didn't want to give it another go and that I would move out and he could keep the house.

I wanted a small wedding with just our close family and friends, and I didn't fancy getting married in Ireland tottering up the aisle, so we decided to get married abroad. Mattias remembered what I said about the Caribbean and how I always wanted to go there so he surprised me and said we were going to the Caribbean to get married.

And the rest, as they say, is history.